He was so mesmerized by her delicious brown eyes and silky skin that he'd lost track of where he was.

"I still don't know anything about you," she said again.

He ran his tongue between suddenly parched lips. *I'm the town drunk's son. I'm a drifter, a would-be-musician…and I'm not good enough for you.* So far, he hadn't lied to her, just sort of hinted at some stuff and let her draw her own conclusions.

He hadn't told her about combing bars for his dad, or coming home to find the electricity off because bills hadn't been paid, or the humiliation of finding his father passed out on the floor. A girl like Madelyn would never understand a world like that.

Dear Reader,

Okay, it's about time: the token guy finally gets his story! This month, we try and delve into the mind of that interesting species: the tortured, creative man. You know the type—they brood, they *think deep thoughts,* they never commit....

And they're a lot more interesting than that office-type Mom has been trying to get you a date with for years. ("I don't know why you won't give him a chance. He's so *nice*.")

I mean, look at me, I ended up with a loner, a brooder, a thinker. I passed up "nice" and I've even lived to tell the tale. (So far.)

Enjoy—

Lucia Macro

Senior Editor
Silhouette Books

Please address questions and book requests to:
Silhouette Reader Service
U.S.: 3010 Walden Ave., P.O. Box 1325, Buffalo, NY 14269
Canadian: P.O. Box 609, Fort Erie, Ont. L2A 5X3

Getting Real: Christopher

KATHRYN JENSEN

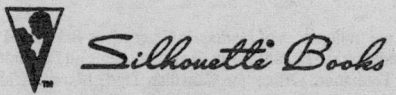

Published by Silhouette Books

America's Publisher of Contemporary Romance

If you purchased this book without a cover you should be aware that this book is stolen property. It was reported as "unsold and destroyed" to the publisher, and neither the author nor the publisher has received any payment for this "stripped book."

 SILHOUETTE BOOKS

ISBN 0-373-20203-2

GETTING REAL: CHRISTOPHER

Copyright © 1994 by Harlequin Enterprises B.V.

All rights reserved. Except for use in any review, the reproduction or utilization of this work in whole or in part in any form by any electronic, mechanical or other means, now known or hereafter invented, including xerography, photocopying and recording, or in any information storage or retrieval system, is forbidden without the written permission of the editorial office, Silhouette Books, 300 East 42nd Street, New York, NY 10017 U.S.A.

All characters in this book have no existence outside the imagination of the author and have no relation whatsoever to anyone bearing the same name or names. They are not even distantly inspired by any individual known or unknown to the author, and all incidents are pure invention.

This edition published by arrangement with Harlequin Enterprises B.V.

SASSY is a registered trademark of Sassy Publishers, Inc., used with permission.

® and TM are trademarks of Harlequin Enterprises B.V., used under license. Trademarks indicated with ® are registered in the United States Patent and Trademark Office, the Canadian Trade Marks Office and in other countries.

Printed in U.S.A.

WHO'S WHO

C. J. CLARKE:
The imperfect daughter in a perfect family. She's left her past behind, determined to be a success, but discovers that fame and fortune are *not* to be found at TV station WZZZ.

JESSICA MONTGOMERY:
When you're blond and beautiful, people tend to think you're a bimbo, but Jessica is determined to show the world that there is more to her than just another pretty face.

CHRISTOPHER McGUIRE:
Bartender, guitarist with a local band...determined to hit the big time any way he can. Can have any woman he wants when he wants—except for the one he *really* wants.

BECKY DELANEY:
Fresh off the farm, she comes to the city to find some excitement, and has to learn the hard way that when you're looking for trouble, you usually find it.

MADELYN PHILLIPS:
Pretty, perky, smart and perfect. So what was she doing with Christopher? And what would happen to her if he broke her heart?

One

The radio-alarm clicked on, and Neneh Cherry belted out a pop-lament on urban violence at a couple of thousand decibels. Christopher McGuire rolled over in bed and slammed his hand down on the snooze button.

"No-o-o!" he groaned, pulling the sheets over his unshaven face.

It couldn't possibly be morning. Hadn't he only just gotten to sleep? Sometime after 2:00 a.m. his band had finished their second rehearsal of the day. Chris, their lead guitarist, had dragged himself home to his apartment—only then remembering that he had a chapter to read for English class the next day. Correction... that morning!

He couldn't remember what the chapter had been about or when he'd crashed. He felt like hell, his eyes stung and his head ached dully. An uncomfortable pinch around his hips told him he'd fallen asleep in his jeans—*again*.

A couple of minutes later, as he was drifting back to sleep, the deejay blasted him straight up in bed.

"Good morning, Chicago! It's a sunny sixty degrees in Loopland at 7:13 on this manic Monday! We've got your favorites lined up for the next hour—"

Chris reached over and shut off the radio. "Seven-thirteen," he muttered, hugging the pillow that smelled of his own skin and two weeks of unwashed linen. "Gotta get to class... by eight-thirty...."

Opening his eyes just wide enough so he wouldn't trip over the piles of dirty clothes, sheet music, old newspapers

and CDs strewn across the floor, he staggered into the closet-size bathroom of his studio apartment. The face reflected in the medicine chest stared groggily back at him as he stripped off his flannel shirt, popping a button. Trapping it under a bare foot, he dropped the button into his chest pocket.

Chris splashed cold water on his face then cupped two handfuls over his longish black hair. He retrieved a comb from the cabinet, dragged it through the damp strands around his forehead and chiseled jawline. Bare-chested, his jeans slung low on his hips revealing his hard, flat stomach, his hair dripping—he looked like a darker version of James Dean, or a leaner Matt Dillon. A single gold stud pierced his left earlobe. Otherwise, he wore no jewelry.

Chris decided against shaving. No time. But his grumbling stomach told him he couldn't pass up breakfast. Something fast, he thought. A bowl of cereal or toast. But first, clothes.

After pulling open one empty drawer after another in the secondhand bureau and rummaging through the pile of laundry at the foot of his bed, Chris decided to go with the flannel shirt he'd slept in. At least he'd only worn it one day... and one night. Maybe he could find a safety pin to take the place of the button?

But there were no pins in the junk drawer in the kitchen. And as for food—the cupboards were definitely bare. He was out of milk, too. Chris contemplated a couple of handfuls of dry cornflakes and decided that was too gross a way to start the day, even for him.

He hurriedly pulled on his leather jacket, tucked his English text under his arm and was halfway through the front door when he sensed something in his path. A sturdy figure was hunkered over in his doorway.

"C.J.! What are you—" He vaulted over the girl's crouched body to avoid knocking her down.

His neighbor wore an oversize purple sweater and plaid leggings. Unperturbed by their close encounter, she stood up and held out a paper plate piled with brownies.

"I just finished a batch and thought you might like some," she said cheerily. "I was going to leave them in front of your door, but since you're here..."

Chris smiled at her, stuffing his text inside his jacket before she could see it. "That's nice of you, bringing me goodies like this all the time. But I'm in a rush, gotta get going."

C.J. frowned, eyeing the fragrant chocolate mountain in her hands. "I suppose I could keep them for you in our apartment," she offered, "since you just locked the door."

"That would be great."

Her eyes dropped to the opening of his black leather jacket.

"One of your shirt buttons is missing," she observed.

"Yeah, got it in my pocket. Don't have time to fool with it now."

C. J. Clarke had nursed a crush on him since the day she and her roommates moved into the apartment across the hall from him. But now she was dating David Griffin seriuosly. Chris was glad for her. She *was* a sweet girl, but definitely not his type. C.J. would be perfect for a steady guy like David, but not for a wandering rocker with an uncertain future. Some old habits died hard, though, and C.J.'s mothering instincts still came out in full force.

She stood between him and the elevator. He weighed his chances of escape.

"Look, C.J.... I really gotta run," he said, stepping around her. "And I don't want you to bother—"

"It's no trouble at all!" She laughed. Clamping a hand on Chris's jacket sleeve, she yanked him unceremoniously across the hall and through the door of her apartment.

"Sewing a little button on will take two minutes, and you'll be all set for the day."

Becky Delaney and Jessica Montgomery, the two girls who shared the apartment with C.J., dashed across their kitchen in nightshirts. Becky's hair was in electric curlers, and Jessica looked fresh from the shower, her long blond hair wrapped on top of her head in a fluffy towel.

"Hey, guys, look who's here!" C.J. sang out happily.

Becky's pale skin turned three shades paler. "Oh, hi, Chris. You're up early." She grabbed an orange from the refrigerator and ducked into the bathroom with a bashful wave.

Jessica folded her arms over her chest and coolly observed her roomie. "C.J., don't you think it's a rotten time to entertain? I have to be at the Art Institute in half an hour, and Becky will be in big trouble if she isn't at her desk by nine."

All three of the girls had full-time jobs in the city, although, as far as Chris could tell, their salaries were pretty pathetic. Jessica worked in the gift shop at the Art Institute of Chicago. Becky took personal ads over the phone for a funky alternative newspaper, *Chicago Now*. And C.J. slaved as a production assistant for a local TV station.

Chris opened his mouth to say he'd better leave, but C.J. cut him off.

"Oh, we won't be in your way," she promised happily. "Give me the button, Christopher. Is it in here?"

She fished it out of his shirt pocket and took off in search of a needle and thread.

Giving in to the girl's good-natured helpfulness, Chris strode over to the refrigerator and pulled out the milk carton. He flipped open the top and raised it to his lips before he caught Jessica's disapproving glare.

"Sorry," he muttered, and plucked a clean glass from the dish drainer beside the sink. Grabbing two of C.J.'s brown-

ies, he sat down at his hosts' Salvation Army table with his breakfast.

Jessica poured herself a cup of coffee and took the seat across from him. She cast an irritated glance at her watch then toward the bathroom door.

"Running late?" Chris asked.

"Three girls and one bathroom," Jessica moaned. "It's impossible."

She tore the towel off her head and began vigorously rubbing her long, golden tresses between the layers of terry cloth. Even damp and without makeup, she was a stunning girl, Chris thought.

He liked all three of his neighbors. They were sort of like the sisters he'd never had, and he enjoyed being around them. He never felt pressured to put on a macho or suave front for them, and they'd long ago stopped dashing off to run a brush through mussed hair before letting him in the door. The four dropped in on each other whenever they felt like it.

Jessica interrupted his thoughts with a scream toward the bathroom door. "Hurry up, Beck! I have to do my hair!"

"You could plug in the hair dryer in your room," Chris suggested, feeling a little more awake as the brownie and milk coated his stomach.

"The outlets are all used up—or blocked by furniture," Jessica said.

"Or run an extension cord from the bathroom out here."

She narrowed her eyes at him. "How much does an extension cord cost?"

"Budget still tight?" he asked casually.

"As a spinster in a corset," she said with a sigh.

Unlike the other girls and Chris, Jessica had come from money. Chris imagined there were a lot of things she'd been used to having that she couldn't afford since she'd refused

her dad's offer to set her up in a boutique. She often seemed to have little idea of the cost of necessities.

Becky burst out of the bathroom door, swathed in a brightly colored bath sheet, and rushed into her bedroom, swinging the door closed behind her.

"Thank God!" Jessica cried, deserting her coffee cup to dive for the bathroom.

C.J. exploded from her room. "Wait!"

"It's my turn!" Jessica snapped.

"All right...all right," C.J. said soothingly. "Just let me check in the medicine cabinet for a needle."

A second later, she was out again, triumphantly waving the tiny, bright treasure in front of Chris's face. "See? You'll be out of here in no time...oh, and I see you had time for breakfast. Great!"

He started to shrug out of his jacket, taking care to keep the textbook under cover.

"Don't bother taking off the shirt," C.J. said with a professional air. "I can sew the button right onto you."

Chris observed her doubtfully. "I don't like the sound of that. You're not going to stick me or anything—"

"Don't be silly! I'm an excellent seamstress," C.J. bragged.

Chris sat tensely in the cheap maple chair while C.J. slipped two fingers inside his shirtfront to catch the needle. She hummed softly to herself as she worked.

"There!" she said, after just a few strokes. "Done!"

"That's a great job. Thanks," Chris said, quickly standing up. If he gave her half a chance, he knew she'd come up with another favor to do for him, which would guarantee he'd be late for class.

"See ya 'round," she called after him. "I'll keep the brownies for you till..."

He was already halfway down the hall, her voice fading as the elevator doors squeaked closed.

* * *

The University of Chicago campus was about fifteen minutes by bus outside of the Loop, which was the area enclosed by the elevated train system known as the El, which was where Chris lived. Although the apartment had at first seemed to be in an inconvenient location for a student, Chris had chosen it because it was close to Razzles, where he tended bar, and to the local clubs. Besides, the place was dirt cheap compared to housing closer to campus.

Chris had never had much money. What he did have during his high school days had gone to helping out his dad. As soon as he'd graduated, he'd taken off for New York—his guitar on his back and fifty bucks tucked into his jeans pocket.

He didn't have much luck finding work with a band in New York. The music scene there didn't suit him; everyone his age seemed to be into rap and drugs. After a year he left and headed west, working odd jobs to pay for food and motel rooms on the way, hitching rides when he could. He stayed for a few months in a little town in Missouri, and for another in Abilene and in Albuquerque.

Six months after leaving the East Coast, he arrived in L.A., where he was sure his chances for jump-starting his music career would be better. Unfortunately, he hit the city in the middle of the latest wave of riots, and things went downhill from there.

At last Chris had returned home...well, not exactly home. After living on his own for almost three years, he couldn't bear the thought of sharing space with his old man again. But Chicago was only a few miles from Eldersdale where he'd grown up, and the guys in his old band were still floating around, doing gigs when they could find them. He knew Jimmy and Steve would take him back, and there were so many trendy night spots in the Loop, he was bound to land a job tending bar at one of them.

If his plans worked out and he actually earned a degree from U. of C., he wouldn't have to live from day to day in a run-down apartment, always working pick-up jobs.

For some reason, Chris thought of his mother and how proud she'd have been to see him make it through college. He couldn't really remember what she'd looked like; he'd been only four years old when she died. But he kept a photograph of himself, holding her hand in front of a red wooden park swing, in the top drawer of his bureau. For him she was eternally twenty-four years old—just two years older than he was now. Her sweet smile encouraged him to keep trying, at least in his imagination. Yeah, he'd make her proud of him.

But, better yet, he'd prove to *himself* that he was worth something.

Chris stepped off the Metra bus and jogged across the main quadrangle toward Albert Hall. He had psych later on in the day, and he was ready for that class, having read the chapters and made some hasty notes over the weekend. But English 101 was a required course that he wasn't doing too hot in, and he'd done nothing to prepare for it.

He hoped he could slip into the back of the lecture hall and remain invisible for the next hour.

When Chis reached the auditorium door, it was closed. He listened to Professor Kraig's voice drone on for a few minutes as he paced the deserted hallway. He considered cutting class but figured since he hadn't read the assignment, he'd at least better take notes on what was left of the lecture.

Gingerly, he shouldered the heavy door open.

It took a moment for his eyes to adjust to the dim light. At first it appeared that every seat on the sloping auditorium floor was taken. Then he spotted a chair with a coat lying across it, two rows from the back where he stood.

A skinny girl with straight brown hair and glasses occupied the end seat beside the coat. She was writing a mile a minute on a legal pad.

Picking a second when the Kraig glanced down at his notes on the podium, Chris sprinted down the sharply sloping aisle toward the empty seat. He stepped over the girl's knees, lifted the coat out of his way and hastily sat down.

"Is this yours?" he whispered to her and held out the bulky bundle of tweed.

She jumped, as if surprised he'd spoken to her, then stared at him with a look of horror on her delicate features.

I might as well have said, "Stick 'em up ... your virginity or your life!" he thought, smiling to himself.

"It's the only free seat," he said apologetically.

"Oh ... yes, well ..."

She snapped into action, reaching over to scoop the coat into her lap. Immediately, she turned her attention back to the lecture, but Chris couldn't help noticing how uncomfortable she looked with the coat bunched up in the way of her writing arm.

"I can hold it for you, if you want," he offered.

"That's not necessary," she whispered back at him, keeping her eyes on Kraig.

He shrugged. If she was pissed off because he'd crowded her, that was tough. No one else had two seats.

Chris tried to concentrate on the lecture and on staying awake. Kraig was talking about the classic essay form. At the end of his lecture, he turned up the auditorium lights and started calling out questions to students at random. Chris slid down in his seat.

A few people sitting down front volunteered many of the answers. Most of the others, like him, seemed to be trying to melt into their seats. Monday mornings were rough for everyone.

"Come on, let's hear something from the rest of the class," Kraig encouraged the silent majority.

Chris screened his face with one hand, attempting to look as if he were concentrating very hard on his notes—the few sentences he'd scrawled on the single sheet of loose-leaf he'd remembered to tuck into his text. He didn't mind answering questions when he was prepared, but today was not his day.

"You, in the back with the dark hair!" Kraig's voice wafted over the rows of students.

"Oh, shit," Chris breathed.

He felt the girl beside him straighten up. She cleared her throat. "Thoreau was one of the earliest American essayists," she stated firmly. "*Walden Pond* set a standard in literary excellence for his contemporaries and writers who followed."

"Good," Kraig said. "Any others?"

The discussion continued for another ten minutes, but at last the class was dismissed and Chris felt he could breathe again.

"Your answer was great," he commented to the girl as they stood at the same time to leave.

"It was in the book," she stated.

"Oh, yeah...well...I know." Her five icy words made him feel about as brilliant as an earthworm. He tried to recover. "But I meant, the way you put it. I thought it was a good answer, phrased the way it was."

She stared blankly up at him through long, graceful eyelashes. "I just paraphrased the text," she said stiffly and turned away.

Chris watched her walk up the aisle and disappear behind the swinging door. "Strange," he murmured with a shrug. But there was something about her hasty dismissal of him that tugged at his emotions, something that wouldn't let

him forget about her. And he found himself brooding about her the rest of the morning.

By the time Chris got off the bus in Eldersdale and reached Jimmy Moran's house, it was noon. Jimmy, however, still hadn't hauled his ass out of bed—or, rather, off the basement sofa, which was where he slept half the time.

"Jeez, why do we have to practice so early?" he grumbled, rubbing his puffy face with his fists.

"'Cause your lead guitarist's got to work," Steve Jones, the group's drummer replied. He shoved a mug of coffee at Jimmy.

Chris got busy, plugged his guitar into an amp and started setting up. He'd left his guitar at Jimmy's the night before, to save lugging it into the city and back again.

"It's my night to work the early shift," Chris explained. "Besides, it's noon. You should be up anyway."

"Didn't crash till almost five this morning," Jimmy complained.

"You should have gone to bed instead of taking off to see Cindy."

"Yeah, I know." He propped himself up on one elbow and sipped miserably at the black coffee. "Wasn't worth losing sleep."

"You two fight again?" Chris asked, testing the amps by playing a short riff.

"She wants to get married. Same old crap. I told her to be patient. We gotta make our break first—then we'll be swimming in dough and I can buy her a house and all that crap she wants. The next R.E.M., that's who we'll be a year from now!" He heaved himself up off the sofa and tramped across the unfinished basement with his coffee. "She just can't appreciate my potential!" he cried.

Chris shook his head and smiled as Jimmy disappeared into the bathroom. "Get real," he breathed.

Steve didn't comment, but sat down to warm up his drums, playing them at a quarter volume. He still lived at home, too—in a makeshift apartment over his parents' garage a few blocks away. Neither Jimmy nor Steve worked. Somehow they'd convinced their folks that they needed time to concentrate on their music careers.

Chris hadn't stopped working since he'd gotten his first job delivering pizza coupons door-to-door when he was twelve. He couldn't imagine his old man footing the bill for anything on his behalf—not even food.

"What did you say?" Steve asked after a while.

"When? What?" Chris continued running his fingers up and down the strings of his guitar. The Fender had accompanied him across the country and back again. He kept the slick ebony-and-red enameled wood lovingly buffed to a soft sheen.

"Something about Jimmy."

Chris shrugged. "I just don't think he's being very realistic about our chances."

Steve frowned and held his sticks across one thigh. His jeans had more holes than Chris's. "Jimmy says you're getting an attitude," he said solemnly.

"No attitude. I just don't think he should count on our having a gold album by next summer."

"We're good," Steve protested. His green eyes blinked nervously. "Why shouldn't we be hot?"

"No reason," Chris said. "It's just that I've—"

"You've been *around*," Jimmy interrupted, swinging open the bathroom door. He looked more awake now that he had washed his face. A couple of days' growth of reddish beard shadowed his face. "We know the story. You've seen the East and West Coast music scenes and you've played back-up in recording sessions. Well, let me tell you, that doesn't make you the expert, man!" Jimmy snapped viciously.

"I didn't say it did!" Chris protested. He and Jimmy went so far back, he hated it when they fought. But the blowups seemed to happen more frequently these days.

"No, but you always make a big deal about it," Jimmy said. He picked up a mike and flipped through the sheet music on the table in the middle of the low-ceilinged room. "We've got an important message for the world. We've got things to say in our songs."

"About making the world right," Steve chimed in quietly.

"I know, I know...." Chris moved his guitar too near the mike and feedback screamed across the basement. He turned off his power. "The thing is, *everyone* has something important to say. Bad Trip sings about slums in Queens, Soul Asylum's got a thing about the end of the world, R.E.M.'s into changing the whole world...we all got something to say. That's cool, but we're doing the same stuff hundreds of groups are doing!"

"The thing is, man...we're good," Jimmy insisted, shaking his music in Chris's face.

"Like they're not?" Chris yelled. His anger swelled in his veins. He felt like throwing something at Jimmy, but there wasn't anything within reach except the Fender, and that would be a waste of a good guitar. "Man, you can be so dense sometimes, Jim," he ground out. "Listen, a lot of groups are supertalented. It'll take a hell of a lot of work and luck besides to get to the top! We have to do something besides sit here and play around in your cellar!"

"I told you last night, soon as we get our new bass player, we'll cut a demo," Jimmy promised, suddenly sounding on the defensive. "I wrote a new song—just finished it last night. It's a winner, I swear."

He started to sing it. Chris listened to Jimmy's raspy voice, feeling his body gear down. The lyrics were good,

smoother than some of his earlier stuff. And the beat worked, making the song danceable.

"I like it," he said quietly, when Jimmy had finished. "It might make a really good demo. Meanwhile, you got any jobs lined up for us?"

"There were a couple of possibilities, but I turned them down," Jimmy said, his nose still in the sheet music as he made some notes for changes.

"What?" Chris gasped.

"They weren't our kind of gig, that's all."

Chris couldn't believe what he was hearing. "But they were paying jobs, right? And they'd have given us some visibility."

"We have to be careful we don't get the wrong reputation," Jimmy stated firmly. "These were just high school dances. They want someone to give 'em a beat. Might as well hire a deejay."

Steve looked at Chris and bit his lip but said nothing. They all needed some money to get by on.

Chris couldn't control his anger any longer. "What did you do that for?" he ground out.

Jimmy glared at him. "Listen, we're too good for playing to high school kids. Their little dance committees were auditioning a couple of college bands, you believe that?" he said with a sneer. "Like some education freak's gonna play real music. What a laugh!"

Chris felt as if he'd just been kicked in the stomach with one of his old man's steel-toed boots. "I don't think college is a bad idea, for some people," he said weakly.

"Oh, yeah!" Jimmy laughed wildly, slapping his leg.

Steve nodded knowingly. "College is a place to hide from the real world."

Or to learn about it, Chris thought to himself. But his friends wouldn't understand how much he hungered to ac-

complish. Or how badly he wanted to change just a little part of the world—in his own way.

He was sure he could make a difference for other kids who were growing up the way he had, in what people at school called a dysfunctional family.

Of course, Chris hadn't told his friends about his classes. He was so far away from his goal, it sometimes seemed laughable even to him. But he had to try, didn't he?

"Let's play some music," Chris said tightly. "I gotta get out of here by three."

Two

It had started to rain by the time Chris reached Razzles. Good for business but bad for his leather jacket, which had seen better days.

He used a bar towel to dry it off, then hung it up in Gary's office. Nancy and Rebecca, two of the waitresses, showed up while he was quartering lemons for shooters.

"It's pouring!" Rebecca wailed, straddling a potted plant and wringing out her long red hair over the grateful foliage.

She hadn't worn a jacket, and her fitted jersey was soaked through. Chris enjoyed the view for a while then, with a smile, turned away.

"There are spare clothes in Gary's office, if you want to change," he offered.

"Thanks." Rebecca grinned at him and perched on a stool near the end of the bar where he was working.

She leaned provocatively over the bar. Through the damp pink cotton of her top, he could see the outline of her nipples. He figured she was well aware of the show she was putting on.

"So, what's up with you?" she asked sweetly.

"Nothing you haven't seen before," he retaliated, trying to shock her, and failing as always.

They flirted casually for another fifteen minutes, until the first customers started to file in—searching for a dry spot, something to drink and a sympathetic ear for their complaints about the weather.

Chris served up mostly sodas and beer—a couple of Molsons on tap and plenty of bottled Coors and Heineken. A few regulars ordered shots along with their beers. One girl, who'd come in alone, ordered a fuzzy navel of all things. He mixed the peach schnapps and orange juice, then set the glass in front of her.

"You from around here?" he asked, making idle conversation.

"I work at Marshall Field's, the cosmetic department." She dropped her glance to the glass and sipped thoughtfully. He wondered if she was giving him a chance to look her over.

She had sultry dark lashes and endless legs that extended from beneath her ultrashort skirt. She seemed a lot like other girls who came here. They were sexy and hunting—for what, he'd never been quite sure.

If they were after sex, they usually found a willing partner. At least, few of them left alone. Some stopped by the bar to flirt with the young bartender. Chris wasn't sure if it was him or the job that appealed to them.

For the first couple of months he'd worked in this place, he'd gloried in his good fortune; the reason for it didn't seem to matter. But, lately, the promise of a quick pick-up had started to wear thin.

He considered the cosmetician's professionally applied blush and alluring eye makeup... but ended up thinking of the unblemished, naturally smooth skin of the girl he'd sat beside in the English lecture. But she obviously wanted nothing to do with him, so he shoved her out of his thoughts.

By the time Gary showed, the bar was packed and the deejay was setting up. A dozen more girls had drifted to the bar, chatted with him briefly, then left for more fertile territory when he hadn't immediately asked for a phone number or made any move to set up a date after closing.

"Hey, McGuire!"

He stopped in the middle of handing a customer her drink and turned to his boss. "Yeah?"

"The lady asked for Absolut, not the bar brand," Gary said, motioning for him to give her another drink.

"Oh, sorry...." He made up another vodka tonic.

"Where's your head, man?" Gary asked a few minutes later when he muffed a second drink.

"Somewhere else, obviously," he muttered.

A pretty brunette shot him a speculative look and took a seat on the end stool. He felt like saying to her, *Don't waste your time, I have someone else on my mind. Someone really special.* For the girl from English wouldn't leave his thoughts alone.

Gary rolled his eyes. "I don't know how you do it," he said under his breath. "It's like they throw themselves at you." He leaned over and sniffed Chris's neck. "You got on some special cologne or something?"

Chris laughed and pushed him away. "Hey, cut it out!"

"I'm serious, man. I may not be twenty-two anymore, but I'm not a bad catch at thirty-one, the sole owner of a trendy bar."

"True," Chris agreed.

"I work out. I eat right. I shower and brush my teeth before coming to work, so what's wrong?" Gary lamented. "I have to work my tail off to get a spark of interest from a chick."

"First, don't call them chicks. That's out," Chris advised.

"Gotcha...no chicks. Broads?"

Chris shook his head, grinning. "Not politically correct for the nineties."

"Whatever... Anyway, I have to drop all sorts of hints about how I own the joint and my old man is rich as Midas—not the muffler king, the other—and what do I get?

Your discards, if I'm lucky." He collapsed dramatically against the bar. "It's depressing."

"Maybe they're looking for someone a little more real, Gary old man."

"Real? What's real in this world?"

That girl in class, Chris thought with conviction. *She was real.*

She'd seemed eloquently thin, barely there beneath her tweed coat as she walked up the auditorium aisle. But what there was of her was at once remarkably solid and precious...like a finely etched crystal vase he'd seen in the window of Cartier on Michigan. She had straight, no-nonsense brown hair. And her eyes were a serious mahogany that—thinking about them now—he had liked a great deal. Even as she was snubbing him.

Chris glanced across the bar at the couples just beginning to dance beneath flashing neon lights and white-hot strobes. Some were already testing the waters—touching a stranger's shoulder, then introducing themselves...brushing a hand along an arm while still dancing apart...recognizing someone they'd met a couple of weeks ago and hugging as if they were old friends. The air was filled with the promise of sex, if not romance.

That girl made him think of romance, the old-fashioned kind with long walks and deep conversations, something he'd never had before. He wished he'd gotten her name.

It was after 2:00 a.m. when Chris stumbled into his apartment. His head vibrated with the sound of the music blasting in the bar. With only a couple of hours' sleep the night before, he felt as if he'd been run down by the El and dragged along the screeching rails for ten blocks; every inch of his body ached.

At least I don't have classes tomorrow, he thought.

A sharp pang of disappointment sliced through him. He froze, staring into the bathroom mirror in the middle of brushing his teeth, and he wondered why the promise of being able to sleep the next morning troubled him so much.

It's her, a voice inside him said.

He wouldn't have English class, which was Monday, Wednesday, and Friday mornings. He wouldn't have a chance to see *her* or find out anything more about her. A wave of disappointment washed over all other thoughts, and a cold ache seized his heart. Stripping down to his briefs, he dropped miserably into bed.

The sound of traffic, a police siren somewhere nearby, and an urgent plea from his kidneys woke up Chris. He ran to the bathroom then stumbled blindly back to bed. The radio-alarm, which he'd intentionally not set, read 9:02. Still early. He could go back to sleep for an hour and have plenty of time to work on his assignments before he had to leave for rehearsal at Jimmy's.

But he couldn't sleep.

"Damn her!" he spit out, throwing off the covers.

As he jerked to his feet, he caught a flash of the telephone. The secondhand answering machine/phone he'd picked up at Goodwill was blinking. He scratched his head, staring at the machine. As tired as he'd been, he still would have heard a call come in. It must have already been on the machine the night before when he'd gotten home.

He hit Play and waited while the thing rewound with a sick, grinding noise.

"Hello, kid. Just wanted to see how you've been doing," an all-too-familiar voice said from the machine. "Haven't seen much of you lately. Give me a call when you can."

The voice stopped. Chris stared at the machine, an icy spot growing in his stomach and spreading out through his limbs until he felt chilled all over.

It was his old man, and something was wrong.

He wouldn't have called otherwise. On the other hand, his dad was sober, which was a rare phenomenon. Generally, he only called when he was in a sloppy, sentimental mood brought on by a pint of liquor.

Chris slowly reached out and touched the rewind button. He thought about calling his father. He thought about not calling him. He didn't want to talk to him, but he knew he should in case something important had come up.

Reluctantly, Chris sat down on the edge of his bed and punched in the Eldersdale number. Since it was after nine, his dad would probably be at work, but at least he'd have tried.

Someone picked up the phone after the third ring. "Hello?"

"Dad? That you?" Chris asked.

"'Lo, Chris...yeah, what's up, kid?"

"You called me last night. Is anything wrong?"

"Wrong? Naw...just wanted to hear your voice."

Chris sighed. He didn't believe a word of it. "Dad, why aren't you at work?"

"Well, I wasn't feelin' too hot this morning, tell you the truth. So I thought I'd better call in," his father said.

"Do you have any sick time left?" Chris asked.

Jake McGuire had been working at the paper mill for only three months. He hadn't kept any job for more than a year, for as far back as Chris could remember. And he was rarely at one job long enough to earn benefits.

"Sure, I got days!" his father snapped. "You think I can't count or something?"

"Of course you can count. It's just that—" Chris ran his fingers through the shock of black hair falling over his forehead. Hell, why couldn't the guy lay off the freakin' booze? "Dad, be straight with me. Have you been hitting the bottle again?"

There was a long silence.

"Dad?"

"I'm disappointed in you, Chris."

"Dad, I'm serious—don't pull that crap on me."

"I'm serious too," Jake McGuire insisted. "I've worked hard all my life. If I'm sick, I'm sick. I deserve a day off now and then."

Chris sighed. "All right. So you're sick. Is it serious?"

"Naw, nothing a day or two restin' won't fix."

"So, why did you call, Dad?"

"Oh, yeah, that. Well, I was wondering if you had a little bit to help out on the rent this month. And I know what you're gonna say," Jake put in before Chris could remind him that he'd mailed him a check the first of the month. "I was going to use that money you sent for the rent, but the fridge gave out on me, and I had to get it repaired. I'm just a little short, that's all."

"How short?" Chris asked through gritted teeth.

"Like maybe three... four hundred."

Chris winced, thinking of the money he'd put aside for next semester's tuition. But if he didn't make the modest payment, his dad would lose the house, and he didn't want to think what that might mean for either of them.

"I'll bring it by tomorrow. Okay?"

"Aw, that's great, son. But you don't need to make the trip out from the city. I know you got a lot keepin' you busy. Stick it in the mail. It'll get here in time."

Chris closed his eyes and took a deep breath, trying to loosen the rock-hard knot in his stomach. If only his father were as concerned for him as he pretended when he was getting his way.

"Sure, Dad," Chris murmured. "Take care of yourself."

"Always do!"

The line went dead. Chris held the receiver in his hand, staring at it as the dial tone vibrated against his palm.

"The truth of the matter is, Dad," Chris whispered, "you blew the rent on booze, like always. Why can't you just admit it?"

So why are you sending him your tuition money? a voice chided from somewhere inside Chris.

Because, he answered himself, *I can't let my old man get thrown out on the street.*

On Wednesday, Chris got up a half hour earlier than usual for class. He threw himself into the shower and shaved, then, still naked, crossed to his closet. A few shirts he'd gotten as Christmas presents and never worn hung on the long rack.

On the top shelf were a pair of Levi's, with the label intact. They'd come with the apartment, along with a few beat-up cooking pans, some flour, rancid salad oil and two boxes of stale cereal. He'd thrown out the rest but kept the jeans since they happened to be his size. Folded up beside them was a blue-patterned cotton sweater that Jessica, C.J., and Becky had chipped in together to buy for his birthday.

Chris found an unopened package of Jockey underwear in the bottom drawer of his dresser, where he'd left it for an emergency. He decided he'd have to do laundry after class that day if he was to have anything clean to wear after tomorrow.

Wednesdays and Fridays, English met as smaller groups in regular classrooms. Chris had a vague feeling that the girl from the auditorium was in his section. He could almost picture her floppy tweed coat flung over the back of a writing chair—but, then again, that might be just wishful thinking.

An hour later, as he walked into the classroom, he was struck by the queer feeling that he might be just as screwed

up as his old man. He was about to do something he knew would be bad for him. He was going to walk up to a girl who'd shown absolutely no interest in him. And she was going to tell him to get lost.

But he couldn't stop himself. The more Chris had thought about her in the past two days, the more she'd intrigued him. She wasn't as plain as he'd at first thought. He now pictured a subdued girl who was really quite attractive in a nonflashy kind of way.

He walked in and looked around, afraid she wouldn't be there, then terrified when he spotted her seated near the middle of the room, scratching away on a legal pad. His heart thudding in his chest, he walked over and stood in front of her.

"Hi," he said, an octave too high. He cleared his throat and tried again. "Hi," he repeated, kicking himself when he sounded like his own echo.

"Hello," she said softly, without looking up from her notes.

Chris quickly sat in the chair beside her, even though he'd normally sit farther toward the back. He introduced himself. I'm Chris McGuire. I didn't catch your name the other day."

She lifted her head and gazed at him steadily through the lenses of her tortoiseshell glasses. Her eyes were a warm, rich brown that reminded him of C.J.'s brownies, melty and steaming from the oven. She smelled like soap and baby powder. Chris suddenly felt like a blob of Jello-O, incapable of stopping himself from sliding out of his seat and dissolving into a puddle on the floor.

"I'm Madelyn," she said formally. "Madelyn Phillips." She turned quickly back to her notes.

Gritting his teeth, Chris tried again. "Studying for the test?" he asked.

Her head shot up, and she stared at him, her eyes wide with horror. "*What* test?"

He tried to keep a straight face, but failed. "Just kidding. We don't have another one for three weeks—that's the midterm exam."

She closed her eyes softly and let out a long breath. "That wasn't very nice to tease me like that."

"No, it wasn't. How about letting me make it up to you, Madelyn?" He liked the way her name felt on his tongue. It tasted refined, the way she looked. She was probably from some snooty old-money Chicago family that brunched Sundays at Le Français and took long winter sojourns in the islands.

So, why are you messing around with her?

Because I like her, he decided. I like her a whole damn lot.

"You don't have to do anything," she pronounced demurely. "I just wish you hadn't said that . . . about a test."

"No, really," he said hastily. "I want to make it up to you. How about we go for a cup of coffee after class?"

She peered at him over the rims of her glasses, and he couldn't help thinking how deliciously sexy she looked because she wasn't even trying to flirt.

"No, thank you," she murmured.

"Well, something else then . . . you name it."

"I can't go for a drink," she explained coolly. "I have to go to Harper Memorial and research a paper."

"Hey, talk about coincidences!" He beamed at her. "I was heading over to the library myself, right after class. We can walk together."

She studied him suspiciously. "I've never seen you there before."

"I'm usually in one of those little cubbyholes on the second floor."

"A carrel?" she asked.

"Yeah, that's the place." He felt dizzy with success. He could tell she was about to give in! "Anyway, maybe we could find a table, and I could help you dig up the books you need. Then we could review the English assignment together."

Madelyn drew the tip of her tongue delicately across her top lip. "I study alone. I get more done that way."

"Oh." He took a deep breath, wondering how he could have been so wrong. "Well, some other time, then. That's cool."

Slumping in the chair beside her, Chris opened his book but felt too frustrated to read. A minute later Professor Kraig walked in and began class.

For the next forty-five minutes, Chris couldn't keep his eyes off of Madelyn Phillips. The way she held the pen with her little finger gracefully curled... the way she tilted her head to one side as she listened raptly to Kraig... the way she sat, slim and straight in her chair, intent upon everything around her—every little habit seemed to tug at his heart.

But she doesn't like you! he reminded himself. It was probably his clothes or that the black leather jacket didn't stand up to her smart plaid wool skirt and tan, jewel-neck sweater. His heart sank, and he felt as if every breath he drew was a painful chore.

At last class was over. Dejectedly, Chris scooped up his notepad and books, and started for the door. He got caught behind a traffic jam of escaping students, then felt something brush his shoulder from behind.

Chris turned to find Madelyn looking up at him with a timid, half smile. "I guess it would be sort of silly for us not to walk together, since we're going the same place," she murmured.

A slow grin spread across Chris's face. Maybe he had a chance after all. "Great! Let's go— Oh, wait."

"What's wrong?" she asked.

GETTING REAL: CHRISTOPHER

"I've got to call someone. My, um, my dad..." he improvised wildly. "Do you mind holding on for two minutes?" He couldn't very well tell her about his band. A classy girl like Madelyn wouldn't think much of a rock guitarist who was taking a measly six credits in his spare time.

"Not at all," she said. "There's a pay phone under the stairwell. I'll wait for you by the back door."

"Great!" He had to swallow the impulse to scream for joy. "Be right back."

Chris flew along the corridor and down the stairs to the pay phone. He dropped in a quarter and punched seven digits.

"Yo!"

"Jimmy?" Chris asked.

"Yeah, man, what's happening? We're all set up, just waiting on you. Got a new bass player to try out, too."

"Hey, that's cool." Chris took a deep breath. "Say, I'm not gonna make practice today. Something came up."

"Came up?" Jimmy echoed. "What are you talking about?"

Chris had never missed a practice, even when they disagreed on the material or what gigs to take. Jimmy seemed to be having trouble comprehending the unfamiliar situation.

"Yeah, I can't explain now. See you tomorrow, okay?"

He hung up before his friend could ask any more questions.

Three

Madelyn waited nervously outside in the quad. The sun shone brightly, but the wind was strong, making the fifty-degree temperature feel at least ten degrees colder. She started biting her nails; then caught herself and stopped. A queasy feeling nipped at her stomach, and she drew a deep breath, hoping to calm her somersaulting nerves. Nothing seemed to help.

As she watched Chris step outside the building, look around, then start toward her, she asked herself the same question that she'd been asking ever since Monday in the auditorium: *What on earth does this guy see in me?*

At first, his choosing the seat she'd draped her coat over had seemed pure coincidence. After all, chairs were scarce on lecture hall days; if you came in late, you took a chance of getting stuck standing at the back. But then Chris had chatted her up, and today he'd made a point of introducing himself.

When he'd at first tried to arrange to tag along with her to the library, she'd actually looked around the room to see if his friends were hiding in a corner, egging him on and watching to see her reaction. *This has to be a practical joke,* she told herself. What would a cool guy like Chris see in a dorky English major who preferred wool skirts and blouses with Peter Pan collars to jeans and slinky ten-button jerseys?

She didn't know anything about him, but she'd drawn some pretty logical conclusions the first time he'd sat beside her.

He partied hard—looked like he'd been up all night. He rotated girlfriends frequently, probably rode a Harley to class—didn't all guys who wore a leather jacket? He split rent on a dumpy apartment with three other guys just like him. His favorite music was by an in group like Pearl Jam. He knew all the popular hangouts in the city, and never, ever got sweaty palms when meeting a girl.

Her hands had sweat oceans all during class.

And now, here she was, waiting for him to join her and study. There had to be a catch. What was a cool guy like him really after?

She turned on a smile as he strode over to join her. "Your dad okay?"

"Oh, sure," he said quickly, sounding a little uncomfortable. "We just like to keep in touch. We're real close, Dad and me. Let's cut across the quad. If we hurry, we'll beat the crowd and be able to get a good table."

Madelyn nodded tightly. She felt as if she were holding her breath all the way across campus and up the gray granite steps of the library. On the second floor of the immense building, Chris stopped beside a table with books scattered over its top. He moved them aside.

"This one okay?" he asked.

"Fine," she said, putting down her knapsack with a too-loud thud. She pulled ineffectually at the sleeves of her coat.

Chris helped her off with it and laid it over one of the chairs. She sat, he took the seat beside her and she felt suddenly in danger of hyperventilating. Forcing herself to take shallow, even breaths, Madelyn opened her book and stuck her nose deep into it, to discourage any further conversation. If he touched her—even to tap her on the shoulder—she was sure she'd scream.

For what seemed forever, they didn't speak. Then Chris asked, "Do you like Kraig's class?"

She nodded. "Yes."

"Are you doing well in it? I mean, the quizzes and all?"

There was a nervous catch in his voice, and she looked into his dark eyes, surprised to see her own timidity mirrored there. Could it be he was just as nervous about being around her as she was around him?

He gave her a friendly smile, and she sucked in a deep breath for courage. It wouldn't hurt to be polite. "I'm doing okay. I think he's a really good instructor," she stated. "His lectures aren't just reruns of the text chapters."

Chris nodded. "You're right. I hadn't thought about that."

"Listen," she said softly, "I really do have to find some books for a paper. I like talking to you, but I..." She smiled apologetically.

"Oh, sure," he said quickly, "I didn't mean to keep you from your work. Hey, do you have a list or anything? You know, books you need to look up?"

Madelyn reached into her book bag. "Right here."

He took it from her. When his fingertips brushed against hers, she felt an electric zap run between them. Her glance shot to his face, but there was no sign in his eyes, as he concentrated on her paper, that he'd noticed.

Chris studied the list for a minute, then pulled a pen from his shirt pocket and jotted down a few abbreviated titles on the palm of his hand. "I'll look for the first five, you can hunt up the rest. Okay?"

An interesting feeling feathered through her stomach. It was nice to have someone take an interest in her work and offer to help out, but it was more than that. Madelyn felt dangerously drawn to Chris McGuire. She decided it was going to take her a while to sort out her feelings about this guy.

GETTING REAL: CHRISTOPHER

* * *

Madelyn took the elevator to the fifth floor of her dorm. Getting out of the creaking box, she stepped over a microwave oven and two suitcases blocking the doors. Obviously someone else had dropped out and was going home; it happened almost every day. The pressures of college were often overwhelming, and not everyone could hack it.

Sandy was blow-drying her hair when she walked into the room. Madelyn stopped and stared at her. "What did you do to yourself?" she gasped.

Sandy pursed her lips and stared at herself in the mirror as she shut off the dryer. "Got a haircut. You like it?"

"I...I don't know," Madelyn said softly.

When she'd left for class that morning her roommate had wispy blond hair that breezed over her shoulders. Now it had been shaved to less than an inch all over her head, except in the front where it fell in shiny bangs over her startlingly blue eyes.

"You hate it!" Sandy accused. "Why can't you just say so?"

"I don't, actually, that is...not really hate it," Madelyn said, scrunching up her nose. "It's just that it's such a drastic change."

"I needed a change," Sandy bit off.

Madelyn's heart went out to her. "Robbie?"

"Don't ever mention his name to me!"

"Okay, sorry."

"He's such a loser. We'd been going together for almost a year. A year! So off he goes to grad school at Penn State, and the next thing I know, I hear from a stranger that he's engaged to some bio major!"

Madelyn sat down on the bed, smiling softly. She might as well let Sandy get it out of her system. While she listened to her roommate's diatribe against her former boyfriend,

she started unpacking her books and pulled an unfamiliar Bic pen from her backpack. Must be Chris's, she thought.

"That wasn't a very tactful way of breaking the news to you," she commented, rolling the plastic tube dreamily between her fingers.

"Tactful? Rob doesn't know the meaning of the word! I don't think he would have told me at all, except I called him and some girl picked up the phone."

"That's terrible!"

"Yeah. I asked who was speaking, and she goes, real snottylike, 'This is Marsha Brown, Robert's fiancée.'"

Madelyn shook her head, trying to look sympathetic. All she could see was Chris, gazing after her with fierce intensity when she'd left him on the library steps. He'd said he had to leave at four-thirty, but asked her to meet him tomorrow for another study session over at the student center. She'd quickly refused. She didn't know any more about him than she'd known before they walked to the library, but she was certain he couldn't really be interested in her.

If he'd been totally ugly and dorky, or even a little stupid, she'd probably have agreed to another study date. Why not? He'd be no threat to her! But she'd found herself liking Chris as they sat, quietly reading together, occasionally sharing information from a book. She hadn't let too many boys get close to her, but those she had hadn't worked out very well. She wasn't about to set herself up with a massive hunk like Chris, only to end up another notch on his hormone belt.

A knock on the door startled her out of her thoughts.

"Anyone home? Oh, wow!" Cassie squealed as she came around the corner into the room. She was a slim, black girl with huge onyx eyes that made her look as if she were always spaced-out on something. "*Love* your hair!"

"Do you really?" Sandy asked, still frowning into the mirror.

"Yeah, sure. You look like a model I saw in *Cosmo*. You think Rob will like it?"

Sandy gave her a drop-dead look.

"What did I say?" Cassie asked, at a loss.

"Her beloved is getting married, and not to her," Madelyn explained succinctly.

"I don't want to talk about it," Sandy insisted.

Cassie shot Madelyn a look that said, *Fill me in later.*

"So, why are you getting back so late from class?" Sandy asked, flopping down on the bed beside her.

"I went to the library," Madelyn said simply.

"You spend entirely too much time there," Cassie advised. "Go to the student center. You can study and meet guys at the same time."

It was a variation of the same conversation they'd had every day since the beginning of the semester. Other girls in the dorm were forever trying to set her up with some loser. This time, a mischievous voice coaxed Madelyn to shock them.

"Why would I want to meet another guy when I was already with one?" she asked innocently, unable to deliver the line while looking either of them in the eye. She rummaged with fake enthusiasm through her purse.

There was a moment of startled silence, then Sandy squealed. "You had a *date?*"

Madelyn shrugged. "Not really. We're in the same English class and both happened to be going to the library."

"But you sat *together*," Cassie stated firmly, endeavoring to get her info straight.

"Sure, why not?" Madelyn found she was enjoying her minitriumph. Of course she'd never see Chris again outside of class, but that didn't matter. It felt good to act flip and worldly with the other girls, to be one of them for a change.

Sandy and Cassie exchanged meaningful glances.

"What's he like?" Cassie demanded, moving her thick wavy hair out of her eyes.

"Oh, he's a little over six feet tall, has black hair that's a little too long in the back. It touches the collar of his leather jacket. And he has nice eyes—dark with a sparkle in them when he's concentrating."

"Any deformities?" Cassie asked dryly.

Sandy slapped her arm. "Quit that!"

"Well, I was just trying to figure out what's the catch," the other girl complained. "I mean, I think Madelyn is cute and all, but she hasn't gotten a lot of notice from even the moderately good-looking guys on campus, so why—"

"Why should a gorgeous guy like Chris McGuire pay any attention to me?" Madelyn finished for her, suddenly snapping back to reality. "That's just what I've been wondering."

"No shit. He must really be something," Cassie breathed.

Sandy chewed her lip for a moment. "So did he ask you out?"

"Yeah," Madelyn admitted.

"And?"

"And... I said no."

Cassie leapt off the bed. "Why?" she shrieked.

"I just don't think he's my type. Besides, he can't be serious about wanting to be with me. He's got all U. of C. to pick from. Why go out with frumpy little me?"

"True," Cassie said.

Sandy hit her again. "You have absolutely no sensitivity," she scolded.

"I didn't mean anything bad by it," Cassie said sulking, rubbing her arm. "Besides, it really doesn't matter why he wants to date you, Maddie. I mean, it's not like you're committing to him for the rest of your life or anything. Go out with him once or twice. Loosen up... have a good time."

Madelyn considered her advice, then sighed. "But what if I like him? Then he never wants to go out with me again?"

"You mean, what if he breaks your heart after one date? Get real."

Madelyn stared down at her linked fingers in her lap.

"Listen, how long has it been since you've had a real relationship with a guy?" Sandy asked.

"I don't know... six months."

"Six months without sex!" Cassie shrieked.

Sandy rolled her eyes. "The nympho speaks." She turned back to Madelyn. "But she has a point. Your hormones must be just about oozing out of your body by now. It's not the worst thing in the world to crawl into bed with a hunk for a one-nighter. Practice safe sex and all that, but have a good time. It's what I intend to do the first chance I get," she finished wryly.

"And if he's nice, it'll be even better," Cassie added, giving her a sisterly squeeze.

Madelyn looked at her, then at Sandy. "But he's so cool and great looking. And I'm so... ordinary." She hesitated. "I can see either of you with Chris before I could imagine me with him."

"So how do I get to meet this Chris-god?" Sandy asked smoothly.

Suddenly the thought of setting Chris up with any of her friends sent an unexpected wave of nausea through her stomach. She didn't want to imagine anyone in his arms... anyone but her.

"Forget it," she said quickly. "I saw him first."

Friday seemed to take forever to arrive. Every other hour, Madelyn lunged for her closet and started pulling out clothes. Her pleated navy blue skirt looked too preppy. The tartan plaid skirt and embroidered white blouse her mother had given her last Christmas was just too prim. Even the

trendy, brown-and-cream print dress she'd picked up on sale at an expensive department store seemed too unimaginative to impress a guy like Chris.

At last, on Friday morning a half hour before class, Madelyn settled on a retro forties dress she'd discovered at a flea market. It had a black background with delicate white flowers all over it, and the skirt ended demurely at her calves. However, the silky fabric clung to her almost curveless body in a way that, she thought, might look vaguely alluring.

"Dress it down with my boots," Sandy suggested, pointing to her ankle-high, laced black leather boots.

Madelyn tried them on together, then decided to complete the look by twisting her straight hair up on top of her head.

"You look super," Sandy mumbled, still in bed. Her first class was at eleven, and she wasn't in the habit of using her free mornings to study.

Madelyn clasped a silver locket around her throat and let it nestle in the hollow between her collar bones. She figured she was overdressed, despite the clunky boots, but who cared?

She rushed across the quad toward the Social Sciences buildings and arrived two minutes late—something she never did. When she burst into the room, most of the seats were taken. But Chris was already there, and the desk next to his appeared empty. As she squeezed between chairs, she saw him reach out and retrieve a book from its seat.

He saved a place for me...how sweet! Madelyn thought. She was out of breath from her run in Sandy's unrunable boots.

Kraig began his lecture almost immediately. Madelyn took out her legal pad and began taking notes unlike any she'd ever taken before. Normally, she thought about what an instructor said, condensing his words, leaving out the little

jokes and asides before copying anything down. Today she was too aware of Chris beside her to concentrate—the sense of his nearness, the scent of his after-shave, the masculine way he crossed his ankles as he shifted position. Her peripheral vision repeatedly caught him staring at her with a quizzical expression tugging at his lips.

She wrote down everything—word for word—pushing her pen faster and faster, aware that everything Kraig said sounded as if it were in a foreign language, for it made no sense whatsoever. All she could think about was Chris and wonder what he was thinking about her.

She noticed that he wasn't taking any notes, and it finally occurred to her that maybe he was counting on using hers. The idea began to worm its way into her brain, irritating her, arousing her suspicions. Was this what his interest in her was all about? He intended to use her to get through the course with a passing grade. He probably had a girl doing his work in every class he took. Oh sure, she'd heard about that type before.

When class was finally over, she turned to Chris and said crisply, "I see you didn't bother taking any notes."

He smiled at her, his dark eyes shimmering warmly, pulling her in. "Nope. Didn't need to."

She stiffened. "Oh? And how do you expect to pass the test in three weeks?"

He pulled a sheet of paper from his notebook. "The handout Kraig passed out before class...the one he mentioned twice during the lecture. I think he has a couple extras up front, if you want one."

Madelyn blushed and spun away quickly so Chris wouldn't see her cherry red face. She rushed up to the podium and, murmuring a thank-you to Kraig, snatched up a photocopied sheet of paper. As she trudged back down the aisle toward Chris, she frantically scanned the sheet. It was

a thorough outline of the morning's lecture—her six pages of notes efficiently compressed into one.

That was why Chris had been staring at her! It wasn't fascination with her beauty, interest in her stylish new dress or smugness because he'd conned her into doing the work for two. He'd been trying to figure out why she was obsessed with taking her own notes, when Kraig had provided an outline of the entire lecture.

"This...um...will be a big help," she said sheepishly.

"Yeah." Chris shuffled from foot to foot as students streamed past them into the hallway.

Madelyn looked up at him, her heart racing. The last time they'd met, he'd asked her out and she'd said no. If she didn't do something to show she was interested in him, he'd think she didn't like him.

"Are you heading over to the library now?" she asked.

"No," he said. "I can't today. I've got something I have to do."

"Oh." She was more deeply disappointed than she'd imagined she could be.

"But—" he studied her expectantly "—we could get together later for a couple of hours. Maybe around three o'clock? Like for a pizza as a late lunch or early supper."

"Oh, I don't know...." She hadn't expected him to turn a nonthreatening library session into a real date—even if it was in the middle of the day. But if she said no, he might not ask again. And she really wanted to find out more about him.

"If you don't like pizza—" he added hesitantly.

"No!" she burst out. "Pizza's fine. I like pizza. *I love pizza!* Where do I meet you?"

"I'll pick you up, since I'm not sure if I'll be back by three. Do you live on campus?"

"Yeah," she said, her mouth running dry. She moistened her lips. "Ashford Hall, fifth floor. You can ring up from the desk and I'll come down."

"Okay." He grinned at her. "I'll see you about three."

She watched him walk out of the classroom, by now completely empty. Only a minute later did she realize that she should be on her way to the library if she was to finish her research work, attend her other two classes and get back to the dorm in time to see Chris.

She hummed to herself as she strode out of the room, a feather-light tingle singing through her nerves. She felt more alive today than she could remember feeling for a very long time.

Chris caught the Eldersdale bus and arrived at Jimmy's house with his heart still pounding a ragtime beat in his chest. He was going to see Madelyn again!

Yet he wasn't sure what that meant.

She'd been so reserved about accepting his suggestion they go for pizza. Had she accepted just because she didn't want to hurt his feelings? She seemed like that kind of girl—very sensitive, the sort to feel sorry for unfortunate jerks who were barking up the wrong tree. Then, as he was about to pull open Jimmy's door, another thought struck him.

Maybe it was something else. Maybe she was . . . well, she didn't like guys. He was an open-minded person. He knew of girls who were simply more interested in each other's company. That was cool—each to her own.

But what if Madelyn was that way? He really liked being around her. She had a soothing manner about her. He could sit and read with her, just be quiet, and he felt as if his soul were being washed clean of all its troubles.

And she was so pretty.... He hadn't been able to take his eyes off of her during class today. She had the pure, simple good looks of a girl who'd never ruined her hair with

bleaches or her skin with heavy makeup. She glowed from the inside out with a special sort of beauty that he itched to be near. He'd wanted to touch her more than anything!

A shiver ran through him as he thought of that possibility, then of the more realistic notion that he simply didn't appeal to her. Him with his schlumpy old clothes, rocker's hair and moment-to-moment life-style. Him, the town drunk's brat... the boy who'd cut half of his classes in senior year to keep a job so he could pay his old man's bills. Him, who'd hitched to New York with a lousy fifty bucks in his pocket while his classmates were marching in gowns and mortarboards to the tune of "Pomp and Circumstance..."

Sure, McGuire, a classy girl like that's going to fall all over herself for you. Fat, retching chance, man!

"Hey, what are you doing standing out here?" Jimmy asked as he opened the door.

"I just got here," Chris muttered, stepping inside—back to the reality of his own world.

Jimmy's house smelled of greasy eggs and stale breakfast bacon. He followed his friend into the basement studio.

Steve was warming up the drums, and a guy he didn't know was trying out chords on a bass guitar.

"This is José. He's the one I was telling you about," Jimmy said.

"Hey, man," Chris greeted the guy, who had strong Spanish features. "Who you been playing with?"

"Discount Depression," José said. "Before them, MT Nest."

"Good music," Chris observed, trying to be polite. Both of the groups were strictly local and only played private parties and small clubs. But Depression was popular with the college and young professional crowd and probably booked a heavy calendar. José was obviously looking to move up.

GETTING REAL: CHRISTOPHER

"I told him we're looking for a fourth so we can get more into our sound, man," Jimmy said. "We got to get bigger before we make a new demo. Then, the sky's the limit. We got offers coming in all over the place!" Jimmy raved.

Chris looked at José. Before he'd met Madelyn, he might not have given a damn if Jimmy dished out a load of crap to steal some bassist from another band. But she'd had a strange effect on him. He wanted to do the decent thing.

"Listen, man," he said, "if you have a steady gig now, I'd think twice about leaving them."

"Oh?" José said, stopping his fingers on the strings. "Why's that?"

Jimmy shot Chris a warning look.

Chris ignored him. "To be honest, we haven't had a job in months. We're a basement band. With a good bass and the right music, we might get noticed. Jimmy's a damn good singer, and Steve and I have had studio experience. But no one can make you any promises."

José looked at him hard, then slowly nodded. "Thanks. I need the cash more than the glory right now. I got a wife, with a kid on the way."

Chris felt a huge weight lift from his shoulders. "That's great. I hope the baby's healthy."

José smiled, his dark eyes bright again. "Me, too." He started packing his guitar into its case. "Thanks for the offer, Jimmy. Keep in touch, man. I'd like to work with you sometime."

Jimmy stared after the boy as he hefted his guitar and crossed the room to the outside door. As soon as it closed behind the bass player, Jimmy exploded.

"What the hell do you think you're doing!" he screamed.

"Telling the truth. It's not fair to pull someone into the group with a lie."

"I'm not lying! We're going to be great!"

"You *think* we are—that's different."

Jimmy rushed at him, blue fire spitting from his eyes. He shoved Chris in the chest. "You're screwed-up, you know that? You don't *want* to succeed. That's your problem."

"Oh, sure. I want to tend bar and play burnt-out clubs all my life."

"Yeah! I think you do!" Jimmy said with a sneer.

In the background, Steve was noticeably quiet, sitting at his drums, studying his sticks as if searching out suspicious flaws in the wood grain.

"I think you sabotaged us on purpose!" Jimmy shouted, his voice shaking and his fists bunching spasmodically at his sides.

"I have better things to do with my life than play mind games with you," Chris said, turning away.

Jimmy's voice dropped to a menacing growl. "Oh, yeah, like what?" He squinted at Chris suspiciously. "Hey, you aren't planning to skip, are you? You playing with someone else?"

Chris sighed. "No, Jimmy. There's no other group. It has nothing to do with music."

"What, then? What is it that's got you so spooked?"

"Nothing. Let's practice, huh? I gotta leave by 2:30 today."

Jimmy threw up his hands. "Jesus H. Christ, you just ain't taking this serious anymore! First you can't make practice, now you're cutting out early—where's your dedication, man?"

"I can't help it. I have to go to work early," he lied. "Are we going through those new songs, or what?"

Jimmy let out an exaggerated groan. "Fine. We still got a couple of hours." He jerked his thumb at Steve to set the beat. "Do it!"

Four

Chris raced into his apartment, tearing off his jacket as he dashed across the room. He shot a passing glance at the clock radio beside his bed: 2:40. He had twenty minutes to make himself look more impressive than the overworked, underslept bartender/rock musician he was...and get clear across town.

Grasping the back of his T-shirt, he pulled it off over his head, then stepped out of his jeans and briefs all in one move. He turned the shower on hot, then seized a disposable razor and shaving cream from the cabinet over the sink. Standing under the steaming spray, he wiped the mist off the mirror glued to the tiles and shaved so close, his skin burned. He washed his hair twice, rinsing it squeaky-clean under the fierce spray, then soaped himself all over, making sure he got all the tricky crevices...just in case he got lucky and Madelyn— No, that would be too much to hope for, he thought. *Don't even think about it, McGuire.*

When Chris was done in the shower, he stepped out without bothering to grab the towel. He ran, dripping and naked, and tore through the bottom drawer of his dresser...the junk drawer.

Size D batteries...old cassette tapes...condoms...dozens of guitar picks...a spare set of strings...more condoms...

"Where are the freakin' scissors?" he wailed out loud. He spotted orange handles and reached down into a rat's nest of old shoelaces and gold-colored chains various girl-

friends had given him, disturbing yet another condom trove. "Jeez, what do they do in here—multiply?"

With the scissors in hand he dashed back into the bathroom. Luckily, most of the steam had dissipated. He ran a comb through his wet hair and studied the ragged sideburns, shaggy bangs and too-long nape in the mirror. He couldn't do much with the back without risking a truly awful scalp job. But maybe if he just trimmed around the ears a bit... and used the razor on the burns...

Five minutes later, Chris observed the result of his amateur barbering and was pleased. For the finishing touch, he trimmed a half inch off the front, so that when his black hair fell forward, he could at least see Madelyn. He removed the gold earring.

By now he was dry. He found the only pair of jeans he owned that didn't have holes in them—clean, thank you!—and pulled them on, not bothering with underwear. He tucked himself in before carefully maneuvering the zipper up. Slipping on the blue sweater his apartment neighbors had given him, he grabbed his keys and wallet and stepped into unlaced Reeboks before racing out of the apartment at exactly 2:49.

There was obviously no way he could reach Madelyn's dorm in eleven minutes. He had sort of let her know that he wasn't sure of the time he'd arrive, but he was worried she might have forgotten his warning and be angry when he was late. He caught the Metra bus and got off at 56th Street, hoping her dorm wouldn't be clear on the other side of the maze of quadrangles.

Spotting a kid carrying a ton of books, he ran up to him. "Hey, which way to Ashford Hall?"

The boy looked startled. "Is that a dorm?"

"Never mind. Thanks," Chris forced out breathlessly.

He found a couple of girls standing in the middle of the first quadrangle beside a fountain.

"Ashford Hall?" he asked.

They turned with bored expressions, which dropped away and transformed into smiles as soon as they'd checked him out.

"It's straight across the quad, between the bio-science buildings," one said, pointing. "You can't miss it."

"Maybe we should show you, just in case," the other girl suggested, eyeing Chris with interest.

"Thanks anyway," he called out, already running.

He spotted the gray Gothic-style building from a distance and ran full-out for it, arriving in the first-floor lobby, totally wiped.

"Fifth floor. Madelyn Phillips," he gasped at the guy behind the reception desk.

"Want me to ring her?" he asked. "Or are you going up? The elevator still isn't working."

"Ring...ring!" Chris wheezed, wrapping his arms around his ribs to keep them from exploding.

He paced in circles, looping around the lobby, avoiding students who were coming and going and looked at him warily as he huffed and puffed, trying to catch his breath.

"Chris?"

He spun around at the sound of her sweet voice.

"Are you all right?" she asked, looking concerned.

"Fine," he managed to get out fairly clearly. "I'm just a little...short of breath."

She smiled demurely at him, her brown eyes warm with humor. "You didn't have to run. You said you might be late."

"I know." He sucked in one final breath and felt it ease out of his lungs at a more normal rate. "I just didn't want to keep you waiting, in case you were hungry."

"At three in the afternoon?"

"Well, I didn't get to eat lunch, and I thought maybe you..." He let the idea go? She was probably so organ-

ized, she never missed a meal, her six-month dental appointments or anything else.

She was looking at him strangely.

"What's wrong?" he asked.

"Where are your books?"

"Books?" He stared at her blankly for a moment, then smacked the heel of his hand against his forehead. "We were supposed to study."

"Study and eat pizza," she said with a straight face. "How could you forget?"

"I don't know. I was just in such a rush to get over here... the afternoon has been so packed." He shook his head. She must think he was a total rattlebrain.

"Never mind," she said smoothly. "We can use mine. Where do you want to go for pizza? The café?"

He shook off his inertia. "No, unless you want to. I thought maybe Johnny D's. They make their own dough and have a great white pizza."

"I've never tried white pizza," she admitted. "I'm afraid I'm a straight pepperoni girl."

He thought of a crude punch line for her setup, but decided against it.

"You'll like it. Loads of mozzarella, garlic, onions, mushrooms..."

"Sounds interesting," she admitted. "I'd like to try it."

They began walking. As they crossed the campus, Madelyn brought up the topic of English class.

"I'm an English major," she said, "so I need this course as a prereq for most of my others."

"How many credits are you carrying?" he asked.

"Twenty-one."

"You're kidding!" He stared at her. "That's a lot."

"I know, but I want to finish my bachelor's degree as soon as possible and get a student-aid position while I'm working on my master's. I'll probably attend summers, too."

"Wow, that's pretty ambitious," he said, honestly impressed.

She shrugged. "I don't know. A couple of other girls in my dorm are doing the same thing. I'll be twenty next March and got a late start with college. I don't want to spend my whole life in school."

"I know what you mean," Chris said. But he was thinking to himself how nice it would be to just take classes and not worry about working to support himself and pay tuition.

He'd figured that he could get a student loan easy enough, since his dad's income had always been so low—or nonexistent when he was out of work. But he didn't want to owe anyone money, not even the government.

"How many credits are you carrying?" Madelyn asked as they approached 56th Street.

"Me?" He hesitated. He was taking six, but that made him sound like a loafer. "Fifteen," he blurted out. "But I'm thinking of picking up another class next semester."

"And your major?"

"Psych." At least he didn't have to fib about that. It sounded respectable enough. "I want to get into social work, mostly to help out kids with family problems."

She looked at him steadily when they stopped at the corner for the light to change. "That's really nice," she said softly. "There are a lot of messed-up kids out there—drugs, alcohol, broken families..."

"Yeah." He looked straight ahead. "I just thought since..." How could he tell her he'd been one of those kids... that now, for the first time in his life, he felt as if he were making some progress toward a normal life? "I just thought that... that since I'd had such a great childhood—you know, a mom and dad who loved me so much, basically gave me everything I needed—well, it would be nice to help out others who weren't as lucky."

She looked as if she were digesting this new information about him, and he thought she looked at him a little differently as they waited on the curb.

The light changed. Without thinking about what he was doing, he reached for her hand. They jogged across the street, but as soon as they reached the opposite sidewalk, she slipped her fingers out of his.

Chris decided not to let Madelyn's reserved behavior bother him. She was obviously shy. But she was worth getting to know better. He'd have to find some way to reassure her that he was safe. It must be scary to be a girl these days, he thought, with all the sickos and creeps loose in the world.

They walked into Johnny D's and ordered at the counter, then took their number to a table near the window so they could people-watch. After a moment, Madelyn opened her notebook and began thumbing through it.

"I thought we'd review the last two chapters tonight. That way they'll be fresher in our minds when we have to start intensive study for the midterm."

"Good idea," he said, impressed with her orderly mind. "Hey, what's this?" He reached for a couple of loose sheets that flew free of the notebook as she flipped pages.

She snatched for them, but he playfully pulled them out of range, then waved them tauntingly at her.

"They're nothing—just old quizzes," she said.

He flipped through. "Ninety-five... ninety-one... and, jeez, ninety-nine!" He looked at her. "You're a genius!"

Madelyn blushed. "No, I'm not. I just study hard. It isn't always that easy."

He handed the papers back to her with an air of reverence. "I didn't mean to imply it was, but I've never come within waving distance of an *A*. I'm impressed."

She smiled, looking pleased. "Thanks. Oh, isn't that our number?"

He got up and fetched the pizza, along with a pitcher of root beer because Madelyn had said she'd had a thing for Hires ever since she was a little kid.

She took a tentative bite of a crusty, cheese-gooey slice fragrant with oregano. Then, apparently deciding she liked white pizza, dove in and devoured two more slices before she surfaced for air.

"I've never seen anyone so small eat so much so quick." Chris laughed.

"Nervous energy, I guess. I burn it right up."

He continued to munch on his pizza as she slowed down to nibble her crusts. "So, you're an English major, and you're acing your classes... What are you going to be when you grow up?" he asked with a smile.

She looked at him through her silky, brown lashes. "You'll laugh."

"I swear, not a chuckle."

"We-e-ell..." she began tentatively. "I want to be a writer."

"No kidding!"

"See! I knew you'd laugh," she said in her meltingly sweet little-girl voice.

"That wasn't a laugh. It was an exclamation of surprise."

"Because I don't look like the writer type?"

"No," he said. "Because that's something I can't imagine being myself. But you..." He considered her through a frame of his hands, as if he were a director studying an actress for a role. "No, really, I can see you as a writer. What would you write?"

"I haven't decided yet. I love poetry, mostly the classics—cummings, Frost, the Brownings, Shelley—but I think it's pretty hard to make a living as a poet these days." She shrugged her slender shoulders and looked at him. "Maybe novels. I love using my imagination."

He sat back against the plastic bench and looked at her, soaking up all the wonderful things that were Madelyn. She was so smart and sweet and gentle.... He'd give anything to touch that perfect, clear skin, anywhere on her body.

He leaned forward again and, reaching across the table, softly brushed one finger across the back of Madelyn's left hand where it curled on the tabletop. She flinched, but didn't draw her hand away. She gazed at him steadily across the table.

"What about you, Chris?"

"Huh?" He was so mesmerized by her delicious brown eyes and the silky feel of her skin that he'd lost track of where he was and what they were talking about.

"What is your family like? Your friends? I don't know anything about you."

He ran his tongue between suddenly parched lips. *I'm the town drunk's son. I'm a drifter, a would-be musician, a C-average student... and I'm not good enough for you.*

"I...um, I grew up in the burbs, not far from Chicago. You know, typical bedroom community, working-class neighborhood."

Her eyes sparkled at him with expectation. "And?"

"Well, there was nothing really special about my life. I went to school, got passing grades, wasn't really into sports or anything like that...." Damn, he sounded boring!

"I never was, either," she said. "I was mostly a reader and deep thinker. We were probably a lot alike. What about musical instruments? I took piano lessons for five years, but I was never very good at it."

Chris continued to gently stroke the back of her hand, tracing the delicate web of faint blue veins that showed through her porcelain skin.

"I studied guitar," he said tightly.

GETTING REAL: CHRISTOPHER 57

"Oh, really!" she breathed, her eyes suddenly alight. "I adore Andrés Segovia, and Bach on guitar is absolutely dreamy."

"Oh, y-yeah," he stammered. "They're nice." Of course he knew about the great classical guitarist Segovia from Spain, and Bach was one of those old-time composers his middle school music teacher always spouted off about while Chris was playing air guitar under his desk.

She giggled. "You're so funny... calling Bach nice, like he was some pop singer on the radio or something. So, what is your family like?"

Why did she have to ask so many questions? So far, he hadn't really lied to her, just sort of hinted at some stuff and let her draw her own conclusions. But he hadn't told her about the nights combing the bars for his dad, or coming home to find the electricity off and a truck taking away their living room furniture because the installments hadn't been paid, or the humiliation of bringing home his high school girlfriend to find his father passed out cold on the kitchen floor.

"Well," he began, clinging to facts as long as he could, "my mom died when I was four years old."

"Oh, I'm so sorry!" she gasped, turning over her tiny hand to cup his comfortingly.

Hey, maybe a little sympathy isn't such a bad thing, he thought. But he didn't want to lay it on too thick, make her pity him.

"It was okay, though. I mean, my dad, he was... he was great, the perfect father. And there were always plenty of relatives around to help out."

There had been no one. He'd had to gut out his childhood on his own. But a girl like Madelyn wouldn't understand a world like that.

"Well, that's good," she said. "I'm glad there were caring people in your life. What does your dad do?" she asked.

"Oh, he's sort of a... um..." Think fast, McGuire! "A consultant. You know, he does lots of different things, moves around between jobs... wherever they need him." *Wherever they'll tolerate him!*

"That sounds fascinating," she said, smiling at him brightly. "I'd love to meet him someday."

Chris nearly choked. He pulled his hand away, grasped his glass with both hands and drank deeply of the watered-down root beer. "I don't think that's gonna be possible," he gasped.

She frowned. "Why not?"

"Like I said, he travels a lot. Isn't in town very often."

"Well," she said softly, "maybe the three of us could all have dinner together some night. After all, it's only a couple of hours out of his schedule. I'm sure he makes time to see you anyway."

Chris blew out a long breath. There was no sense making more excuses now; he'd have to come up with something creative later. "Yeah, that's cool." He glanced up at the round-faced clock above the grill. "Listen, I got to go to work."

"Oh, really! Where?"

His mind raced. A girl like Madelyn would never approve of a common bartender. "I wait on tables in this really exclusive restaurant downtown, just to help Dad with my tuition," he added quickly.

"What's it called?"

"Uh, well, Ra-Ramone's... But you wouldn't have heard of it."

"No, I haven't," she said thoughtfully.

"Why don't I walk you back to the dorm," he suggested before she could ask any more questions. "We can talk about you for a change."

They strode outside into the cool afternoon breeze. The air smelled of fall—someone burning leaves, an apple pie

baking—and pumpkins carved into ghoulish faces accosted them from shop windows. With an enormous sense of relief, Chris turned the tables and quizzed Madelyn. She was straightforward about her tastes and opinions.

"Let's see...I like to do cultural things. You know, go to a concert when I can afford it, hang out at the Art Institute—"

"Really? The Institute?" He could actually say he'd been there. Jessica had forgotten her lunch one day, and he'd taken it to her.

"Do you go there often?" Madelyn asked, her eyes sparkling with excitement.

"Well, once in a while. It's nice."

She poked him playfully in the ribs. "There you go again. Nice."

Chris grinned at her. "I guess that's my highest form of praise."

"Well, anyway, I love it there. I also read tons of poetry, adore old movies—Cary Grant, Eleanor Powell, Bogart—and I'm constantly buying books." She laughed, and he loved the sound of her voice—as clear as church bells chiming. "When I was ten years old, I used to spend all of my allowance on Nancy Drew mysteries. My mother teased me about running out of space for me in my bedroom because of my book collection."

"Me, too!" Chris said excitedly. "I mean, except it was my dad. Gee, it's amazing how much we have in common!"

She looked at him and smiled. "Yes, it is."

He wanted to kiss her, right then and there. But he guessed he'd scare her if he came on too strong or too fast.

"All that will probably help your writing," he commented, taking her hand casually in his as they crossed the street.

This time, when they reached the opposite curb, she didn't pull away. *Things are looking up!* he thought happily.

"What about your family life? I bet it was perfect, right out of fifties TV—the Cleavers and 'Father Knows Best' all rolled into one."

She let out a surprisingly sharp laugh. "Hardly! I didn't have a very happy childhood. My parents fought constantly. My older brother and sister ended up leaving home as soon as they could. I was seven years younger than Tracey, and ten years younger than Kevin. I had to wait it out."

He was shocked. How had such a fragile girl as Madelyn weathered such a storm? But he kept on walking, afraid to look at her for fear of seeing the tears he sensed had already welled up in her pretty eyes.

"I'm sorry. It sounds awful," he murmured.

"It was a nightmare," she admitted. "That's one reason I was so impatient to go away to college, but I had to work for a couple of years to save up enough money to get started. And I wanted to go somewhere far away. You see, we lived in Pittsburgh, so Chicago was like another world for me."

"Are they still—"

"Married? No, they divorced at the end of my freshman year of high school, but it was even worse then." She shook her head and gave a stifled laugh, thick with unshed tears. "I was still underage, so they got joint custody. I spent half the year with my dad in Philadelphia, the other half with Mom. I attended two different high schools my last three years. And my parents never stopped harassing each other. If it wasn't a late alimony payment, it was an argument over whether I should be allowed to date, or go on a class trip, or wear makeup. What a horror show."

They'd arrived in front of her dorm.

Chris turned to face her, and couldn't miss the damp trails down her cheeks that she'd tried her best to blot away with her coat sleeve. She blinked up at him shyly.

"I'm sorry. I really did go on about my troubles," she whispered.

"It's okay," he said.

"I usually don't complain like this. I've never really talked about my folks to anyone. Even my roommate, Sandy, doesn't know how it was for me."

Chris was flattered. She'd cared enough about him to reveal the innermost secrets of her past. She'd been honest. He chewed his lower lip, unsure now that he'd done the right thing by covering up his own past.

"Anytime you want to talk," he said softly, lifting his hand beneath her chin. He touched the silky point lightly with his crooked finger and bent toward her slowly.

Madelyn looked up at him through glazed mahogany eyes, still foggy with emotion. For a moment he felt her sweet breath against his lips; then she turned away.

"Not now," she whispered.

A lump swelled in his throat. He could almost taste her kiss on his lips. Almost. He hungered for it.

"I understand," he said as he stepped back, although he didn't.

There had been girls he'd known less time than Madelyn, and by now he'd already been to bed with them! But she was special, he reminded himself. She was worth waiting for.

"See you...." he breathed, continuing to back away from her with reluctance.

"When?" she asked, sounding surprisingly eager.

He studied her expression, unable to figure out what the hell was going on behind those lovely eyes. He thought about his work schedule. Gary had booked him double

shifts all weekend, at his request. He needed the cash to make up for the money he'd sent his father. And his next tuition payment was only a month away.

"Monday," he said. "See you in lecture."

She nodded, her expression still unreadable, and walked away, leaving the natural scent of baby powder and a touch of old-fashioned lilacs in the air.

Five

Chris spun around behind the bar, knocking a bottle of Chivas out of Gary's hand. The bottle shattered on the tile floor, the golden brandy flowing away between chunks of amber glass as Chris stood looking helplessly at the mess.

"What's with you tonight?" Gary demanded.

"Sorry," Chris muttered, picking up a rag. He bent to sop up the mess.

"That's expensive stuff!" Gary complained.

"So, take it out of my pay!"

His boss stared at him. "She must be some number to throw you into this deep a blue funk. What she do, sleep with your best friend?"

"It's not like that at all," Chris protested. "This girl's special—real nice."

"Oh, *that* kind." Gary rolled his eyes as he stooped to help with a sponge. "Listen, don't go on that mind trip. Like she's too good for you or something. No woman's worth it."

"*She* is."

Gary shook his head. "You poor, sick puppy."

"Who's got a sick puppy?" a voice called out.

Chris turned to face the bar. On the other side sat C.J. and Jessica.

"Hey, ladies!" he said, trying to blow off his mood by being ultracheerful. "What can I get you?"

"A white wine for me," Jessica said with a tired smile.

"Same here." C.J. grinned broadly at him. "Did you finish the brownies?"

"Brownies?"

He'd thought she might have been talking about a new batch that he'd never gotten, then remembered the ones from last week. He'd been so wrapped up in Madelyn, he'd left them out on the counter and they'd gone stale. He'd had to throw them out.

"Oh, yeah, they were great. Thanks, C.J."

"If you really liked them, I'll make you another batch tonight before I go to bed."

He laughed. "You'd better hold off. I've got to watch my waistline."

C.J. blushed and shifted uncomfortably on her stool, and he wished he hadn't mentioned anything to do with weight. She was sensitive about her own generous figure.

"Besides," he added quickly, "if I don't have your delicious goodies for a week, I'll appreciate them that much more later on. Right?"

She nodded at him happily. "Right."

"Isn't that Jimmy Moran?" Jessica asked, sipping her wine.

Chris gazed across the dim room at the scowling figure standing near the door with Steve at his side. His friend stared over customers' heads toward the bar, but seemed hesitant to approach.

Chris motioned to him, and Jimmy started over. Steve hung out around the door, looking uncomfortable.

"What's up?" Chris asked above the canned music. R.E.M. was belting out "Stand." Gary was on his oldies kick tonight.

"I gotta talk to you," Jimmy grumbled, his eyes menacing.

"Shoot."

"No. I mean," he said, glancing meaningfully at Jessica and C.J., "like alone. This is serious."

"I'm working," Chris said. "Talk to me now."

He didn't like the look in Jimmy's eyes. Anger boiled under the deep blue surfaces. He wondered if Jimmy had been brooding over the scene with José, working himself up to another confrontation.

"Listen, man," Jimmy said, leaning across the bar and crowding Jessica so that she had to move to a seat on the other side of C.J. "I don't like your attitude. I'm bustin' my balls auditioning bassists, and now Steve's talking about dropping out cause he thinks you're splittin' on us."

"I'll talk to him," Chris offered stiffly.

Jimmy threw up his hands. "Man, it ain't gonna work, you giving us half your life. You gotta be dedicated, gotta believe in us! If we don't make our break soon, it'll all pass us by! Don't you see that?"

"First we have to decide what kind of band we are," Chris pointed out.

"What are you talking about?" Jimmy wailed.

"Are you in the business to save the world...or to save Jimmy Moran?"

"What's that supposed to mean?" Jimmy demanded, his face red with fury.

"It means, you talk a good line, but people will see through you if you aren't sincere. If you're out for the money, start writing dance songs and quit faking concern for the universe!"

"That's a freakin' sell-out!" the singer roared, leaning threateningly across the bar into Chris's face.

Gary moved down to the middle of the bar and stood beside Chris. "This a friend of yours?" he asked solemnly.

"Sometimes," Chris said grimly.

"Then tell him to settle down or he's leaving real fast."

"I'll leave when I'm ready," Jimmy growled under his breath.

Gary pretended he hadn't heard and gave them a little space. Chris noticed that Jessica and C.J. looked pretty worried. He turned to them for an instant.

"He's okay," he told them, "just a little upset."

"Upset?" Jimmy roared. "Listen, I've had it with you, McGuire. You've been lying to me, and I thought you were my friend."

"Lying?" Chris asked, totally confused now.

"Yeah, man. You said you had to split early to go to work yesterday. Well, Steve and me ran into another bass man and auditioned him. He was good, so I came right on over here to Razzles to tell you about him. But you weren't here."

Chris caught a curious look from Jessica. She was eavesdropping.

"I changed my plans," he said in a low voice.

"I guess you did," Jimmy spat. "Well, I ain't gonna let you use us. If you're playing with another group, trying to cut out on me—"

"I told you, it's nothing like that," Chris insisted wearily.

"The hell it ain't!" With a furious bellow, Jimmy drew back his fist.

Chris ducked a fraction of an inch ahead of Jimmy's knuckles. When he came up, both of his hands went for the singer's shirtfront. Chris dragged him across the chrome bar and held him up so that they were eye to eye.

"Don't pull that crap in here!" Chris roared.

He felt the blood pounding in his veins. Nothing in his life seemed to be working out. Not the band, not school, not even the girl he wanted to date, who probably thought he wasn't good enough for her. He gave Jimmy a shake and dropped him unceremoniously to the floor.

GETTING REAL: CHRISTOPHER 67

Gary was beside Chris before Jimmy could scramble to his feet.

A dangerous look flashed across Jimmy's face, and he reached into his pocket. Remembering Jimmy carried a knife, Chris backed off a step. Out of the corner of his eye he could see a hulking figure crossing the room toward them.

"Come on, Jim!" Steve called from the doorway. "The bouncer will toss us if you don't walk. We can handle this later."

Jimmy took a quick look around the room. Everyone in the bar was watching him.

Chris took a deep breath, guessing he should help him save face.

"Listen," he said quietly, "I'm sorry. I want to play with you, but you have to get the act together. Hire a good bass, tell Steve I'm still in and maybe he'll stay. Then decide what kind of band we really have, and get us some jobs."

"You'll come back and practice every day?" Jimmy asked, glaring at him.

"Yeah. I will," Chris promised, not wanting to think about the logistics too much. He'd never see Madelyn again, between practices, school and work; there just wouldn't be any time. But then again, what did it matter? She didn't care one way or the other about him. When he'd tried to kiss her, she'd taken evasive action.

Jimmy gave him a long, hard look and ducked back under the bar to join Steve. "I'll keep my part of the bargain," he said, then pointed at Chris. "You make sure you do the same."

Chris nodded. If Jimmy ever got his head on straight, they could be a drop-dead band.

He let out a long sigh as he watched Jimmy leave.

"Sorry, Gar," he murmured.

"You mix with a rough crowd," his boss commented, drying a glass with a towel.

"Jimmy can be a straight-out guy, when things are working for him," Chris said sadly.

Gary served two mugs of tap beer.

"Well, I'd give a second thought to hanging out with that type. Too unbalanced. He's just as likely to use that knife he was hiding in his pocket."

Chris shot him a surprised look. He hadn't realized that Gary was that observant, but then he had to be on top of potentially violent situations in his business. One unexpected brawl could end up with a half-dozen injured customers and just as many lawsuits.

"You all right?" Jessica asked, when he passed in front of her a moment later. She studied him solemnly, her pretty blue eyes filled with concern.

C.J. leaned over her wine. "He didn't hurt you, did he?"

"No. I'm fine," Chris assured them. "Jim's just pissed off cause I've been skipping practices."

"He shouldn't be that upset if you have to work. It's not your fault," Jessica pointed out.

"It isn't, actually, work," Chris said slowly.

He considered leaving it at that but decided he really needed to talk to someone. The girls from across the hall were the only real friends he'd found in the city.

He turned to Gary. "Hey, man—I'm due for my break soon. Okay if I take fifteen now?"

"Sure," Gary said, signaling to one of the bar backs to come over and watch the register for him while he covered for Chris.

Chris motioned C.J. and Jessica to an empty table away from the dance floor. A dozen couples were dancing to the Red Hot Chili Peppers. It looked like they were having fun, but he wasn't in the mood.

GETTING REAL: CHRISTOPHER 69

The girls took seats with their drinks and patiently waited for him to speak, as if knowing something important was troubling him and he needed space to get his thoughts together.

"The reason I cut practice is, well... time's gotten pretty tight for me. A lot's going down in my life these days."

C.J. glanced at Jessica. "We were just remarking the other day how you're hardly ever at the apartment anymore."

Chris ran a hand through his hair and drew a deep breath. "Don't laugh—but I haven't told Jimmy and Steve that I'm taking some college classes. They're not exactly sold on higher education."

C.J. munched on a pretzel from the dish on the table. "Knowing Jimmy, you're probably understating the situation."

Chris shrugged. "He and Steve figure we're bound for glory, and nothing else matters. They're totally hung up on fame."

"You don't want to be famous?" Jessica asked playfully.

"Of course I'd like it. With fame comes a lot of advantages."

"Like money?" Jessica said, quirking a brow. She knew about money—she'd had it all of her life.

"Yeah," he admitted. "Money would be okay. I could help out some folks."

"Like take care of your old man?" C.J. asked, her tone suddenly serious as she remembered all the horrible things Chris had once told them about his father. "You know you can't be responsible for someone who refuses to take care of himself."

Chris looked at her hard. Sometimes she came off as just a nice girl who liked chocolate too much. And sometimes

she showed everyone just how savvy she was about human nature.

"I know I can't buy him a sober, responsible personality, or make him a prize citizen, but I..." He dropped his head into his hands. "I can't just walk away from my own father! I tried that once. It didn't work."

"Chris," Jessica whispered, laying a gentle hand on his arm.

He looked up at her. "I'm okay. But it's something more than just school. There's this girl."

"Tell us about her," Jessica prompted when he didn't go on immediately.

"Well, she's really great. Comes from out-of-state. She's in my English class. And I really like her a lot."

"So? That's good, right?" Jessica asked.

"I don't know," Chris said. "Madelyn's great, but I can't seem to get through to her. When I'm around her, I try so hard to make a good impression. But I don't think it's working."

"What have you done?" C.J. asked with a weak smile.

"Well, I wore clean clothes to class the other day, and shaved."

"That's a whopper of a start," Jessica said wryly.

Chris laughed. "Yeah, well, it's a stretch for me. Anyway, I told her a lot of stuff to get her attention. Like—" he hesitated, watching the girls' faces for their reaction "—like how my old man is such a great guy and stands behind me one hundred percent. And how I'm a full-time student."

"What! You lied to her?" Jessica yelped.

"Look, why would a great girl like her have anything to do with a loser like me who's trying to be something he's not?"

"You're working at it, like all of us," Jessica said sternly. "That's nothing to be ashamed of."

GETTING REAL: CHRISTOPHER 71

"Sure, like that's supposed to impress a classy girl like Madelyn."

Chris glanced across the room at the bar. He should really be getting back. Almost every stool was taken, and Gary was hustling to keep glasses full.

"What does a woman want, anyway?" Chris groaned in frustration. "I mean, really!"

"Well," Jessica said, tilting her head to one side and gazing solemnly at him. "For starters, there's honesty."

"Lay off, will you?" he snapped, pushing away from the table to stand up.

Jessica stopped him with a hand on his arm. "I'm serious, Chris. If you don't level with her, you haven't got a chance. Sooner or later, she'll find out you've lied to her, and she'll be hurt."

He stared at her. Something in Jessica's tone told him she was right. But how could he face Madelyn with the truth about his life? He was a loser, always had been, and as soon as she discovered that, she wouldn't even share a lousy pizza with him.

Six

Madelyn dashed across 55th Street to the Hyde Park shopping center. Brushing blindly past other pedestrians, she dove into the drugstore. She had a half hour before class, and she had to pick up Tampax and take them back to the dorm before then.

Her period was overdue. She felt miserably bloated and cranky, but more than that, she was bitterly disappointed with her weekend.

When she'd last seen Chris on Friday, she was certain he was going to ask her out. Maybe they'd go to a museum or a concert—something more special that a study date. Instead, he'd tried to kiss her.

Her reaction had been automatic. She'd been so flustered by his unexpected move, she'd blown everything by turning away. Yet what she'd most wanted was to feel his lips on hers!

Madelyn stopped in front of a display of salon-style shampoos and conditioners and stared, without really seeing it. She replayed the moment as he'd bent toward her, his dark eyes pinning her, telling her she excited him, telling her that he wanted her.

As Chris moved still closer, she'd felt a terrifying prickle race up her spine, and her stomach had turned to jelly. Suddenly she couldn't breathe. It was as if she'd been running for miles and miles, and had at last reached her limit. Needing space to catch her breath, she'd turned her head away from him.

GETTING REAL: CHRISTOPHER

Madelyn blinked at the pyramid of pink and gold shampoo bottles. Chris must have thought she found him repulsive.

"Right!" She laughed out loud, then swung around to find a teenage clerk looking over the top of his clipboard at her.

What was she doing—laughing and talking to herself, lapsing into dazes she couldn't snap out of? Since she'd been on her own, she'd managed to keep her emotions, and therefore her life, in perfect control! Life had been simple without warring parents to deal with. Study, eat a meal, take an aerobics class, go to class, study, eat, spend the evening at the library...

Simple... but in a way lonely, too.

Of course, she'd occasionally envied other girls their less-controlled life-styles. But she'd never been interested in barhopping or wild parties. Sandy and Cassie had gone to a rave Saturday night—geared up with XTC, VapoRub and whistles. They'd invited her, promising thousands of young people would show up in a field south of the city. But she'd told them she wasn't interested.

Instead, she'd browsed alone through rooms of stunning art in the Institute. She couldn't miss the women, who'd come with their husbands and boyfriends, strolling contentedly from one display to the next, soaking up the refined atmosphere, enjoying the beautiful paintings and sculptures. The women had whispered comments and sometimes giggled conspiratorially with their mate over a particular piece.

Oh, how she longed for a companion! A soul mate. A man who'd share her interests, be there to talk with her at all hours of the day or night, go places with her and...

"Oh, damn," Madelyn choked out. Huge tears rolled down her cheeks, and she wiped them away with the back of

her hand. "I should...should have let him kiss m-m-m-me," she said with a hiccup.

"May I help you, miss?"

To her embarrassment, the clerk had followed her down the aisle. He stared at her with a concerned expression.

"N-no." She forced a smile and sniffled. "I just have to pay for... that is, I have to find..." She flushed with embarrassment as the boy waited patiently for her to finish her sentence. "Never mind. I'll find them myself."

Madelyn at last located the Tampax, paid for them at the pharmacist's register and tore out the door into the street. Five minutes later she was dashing down the Midway Plaisance that split the campus when she spotted Chris heading toward her. Unable to face him, she turned sharply to her right, hoping to cut behind Ida Noyes Hall and avoid him.

She felt dizzy with confusion. She should have encouraged Chris by letting him kiss her! What was the big deal about that? But maybe she should be just a little angry with him for not calling her anyway over the weekend. Then she remembered the Tampax and her eyes that were probably an ugly red from crying, and realized she definitely didn't want him to see her now!

She rounded Noyes Hall, sprinted down the sidewalk and ran into Chris coming the other way.

"Hey, Madelyn! Taking a shortcut to English?" he asked, a twinkle in his dark eyes.

"I...no," She cleared her voice and dropped her hand carrying the brown paper bag below eye level. "I have to leave something at the dorm before class."

He glanced at his watch. "You'll be late. We only have six minutes."

"Oh."

She looked up at him. He'd obviously just shaved, and he smelled wonderful—musky and mannish. She ached to

stand closer to him, to feel his warmth in the cool autumn air.

"If it's something heavy," he said, eyeing her package, "I'll be glad to carry it for you."

"No! No thanks, it's nothing...light as a feather," she assured him. She just had to ask. "Did you have a good weekend?" She pictured him partying with girls who looked like Sandy and Cassie. How could she complain? She'd kept him at arm's length, hadn't she?

"Went too fast," he commented, taking her arm and moving her along the walk. "I had to work all weekend."

"Really?" she squeaked out, grinning, then realized how inappropriately pleased she must sound and look. "I mean, that's terrible. Ramone's was busy then, huh?"

"Uh, yeah." He looked straight ahead as he walked.

Since she'd freaked out the last time, she decided that she must somehow let him know she was interested in him. She drew a deep breath, forcing herself to be bold. "Maybe I could drop by some night and say hi!" she suggested.

Chris looked horrified. "No! I mean, we're not allowed to have friends around while we're working."

"Oh." Madelyn stared at her feet as she plodded forward, hugging her brown paper bag. What was she doing wrong? She swallowed over the lump growing in her throat.

"Listen!" Chris stepped around in front of her suddenly. "I don't know why you always act so uptight around me, and I don't know what's going on in your head. But I have to tell you what's going on in mine."

Madelyn swallowed with difficulty and stared up into his handsome, chiseled face.

"I didn't mean to scare you when I tried to kiss you Friday," Chris continued. "It just felt right. Madelyn, I like you an awful lot. I wanted to show you how I felt and get closer to you. But I didn't mean to insult you or anything. If you want me to leave you alone, just tell me. Okay?"

She nodded mutely.

He groaned. "Is that a 'Yes, I want you to leave me alone,' or a 'Yes, I'll tell you how I feel'?"

Madelyn smiled shyly at Chris. His sense of humor was beginning to put her at ease. "It's a 'Yes, I'll tell you how I feel about you' nod."

He let out a long, relieved breath. "So? Is it good news or bad?"

Madelyn forced herself to look him directly in his sexy dark eyes. "I like you, too, Chris," she whispered. "I like you a lot."

He grinned fleetingly; then his lips quickly turned downward. "So, why didn't you want me to kiss you? Are we talking about the kind of *like* as in you just want to be friends? You're not attracted to me?" He stepped closer. The wonderful scent of him was almost overpowering. "You wouldn't want me to touch you?" Chris moved one hand up. His callused fingertip stroked the tip of her nose, moved across her lips, and down her chin.

Madelyn's knees felt as if they were going to give out at any second. She'd never openly discussed sex with a guy in her life. With her high school boyfriend it had just happened. And she hadn't felt one way or another about it when they were through.

Chris was being so tactful and gentlemanly, but she found it almost impossible to voice her feelings. He gazed impatiently into her eyes, waiting for her answer, his hand limp at his side now.

"I am attracted to you, Chris," she blurted out before she could lose her nerve. "I...I think you're very...*very* appealing."

His dark brows rose, and he smirked at her playfully. "Really. Appealing...as in sexy?"

She felt the blood rush into her cheeks. "Yeah." Somehow she dredged up another cupful of courage. "What

about you? Was it going to be a brother-sister kiss? Or a—the other kind?"

"The other kind," he said firmly. "I wanted to make you melt in my arms."

The world spun giddily for Madelyn, and she had to turn away from Chris's mesmerizing eyes to catch her breath.

"Madelyn. Look at me," he said.

She felt as if she had no choice in the matter. She obeyed him.

He stood over her, his dark stare more intense than that of any boy... any man she'd known. Maybe Cassie was right. Maybe she shouldn't be so afraid of letting a relationship happen. She sensed that Chris would be a wonderful, experienced lover. Although she'd had one high school boyfriend and a short relationship with a grad student after that, neither of her young men had been terribly inspiring lovers. With Chris, it would be different—she knew that as sure as she knew her birth date.

Besides, was it so wrong to take advantage of the situation? She really did like him. She'd never felt so urgently drawn to a guy from the moment she'd laid eyes on him.

"Listen to me," he said, which struck her as hilarious since she couldn't have done otherwise. "I think you're very special, Madelyn. I want to get to know you better. I promise I won't do anything to hurt you, anything you don't want me to do. But I have to be honest with you, I'd kill to kiss you now... this very minute. Will you let me?"

It was nearly eight-thirty, and students were rushing past them in the last few minutes before the first class of the day began. Strangely, she didn't care if they stared. All that mattered was that Chris wanted to be with her, and he was willing to take their new intimacy at her pace.

"I'd like you to kiss me very much," she whispered, the catch in her voice betraying her fear and excitement.

A spark of desire flashed in Chris's eyes as he leaned forward... until his lips were a fraction of an inch from hers.

"Still time to bale out," he teased, his breath slipping sensually across her trembling lips.

She moistened them with the tip of her tongue. "No way, McGuire," she murmured throatily.

His warm lips feathered across hers for a moment before pressing gently. She opened her mouth slightly, but he didn't deepen the kiss. She reached behind her back to steady herself against a tree trunk. When at last he pulled away, she felt pleasantly light-headed, and every nerve in her body tingled.

"Pretty scary stuff, huh?" he asked, laughing tensely.

She smiled up at him, surprised but also pleased that he'd needed her reassurance. "That was very nice," she murmured.

"Wouldn't mind a repeat performance?" He took her hand from the tree and entwined her arm gently with his behind her back.

"Not at all," she said dreamily. But her glance quickly fled from his. She still had trouble meeting his eyes for long. Mirrored in their dark surfaces was the skinny, plain girl she'd lived with all of her life. The same question still haunted her: *What does he see in me?*

"Good," he said, landing a peck on her nose. "The best is yet to come." Before she could even imagine what that might be, Chris suddenly snapped into action. "Come on, we gotta get going or we'll miss the whole lecture."

Madelyn slipped her fingers from between his and glanced at her watch. "Oh My god! Class started fifteen minutes ago!"

"No problem. We'll sneak in through the back." He winked at her. "I'm good at that."

* * *

She might have attended the lecture in body, but in spirit Madelyn drifted sublimely in her own world, far away from academia. She spent the entire hour whispering like a grade school girl with Chris at the back of the dim lecture hall.

Madelyn confided in him how much she loved spending time at places on campus like the Smart Museum or the Renaissance Society. And she told him about her admiration for the Impressionists, and her lesser delight with the Postimpressionists. As often as she could, she attended the Chicago Symphony's concerts. The Lyric Opera was another place she wanted to go sometime—but tickets were expensive and often hard to get.

She couldn't seem to stop talking, even when a guy seated in the row ahead of them flashed her an irritated look. She felt deliciously out of control! Teeming with vitality! Sandy would have said her hormones were running wild, and she worked them off by talking nonstop.

"When I go downtown, I always prefer to walk," she jabbered on happily, "even though the trip takes only fifteen minutes on the Jeffrey Express..." That way she could walk past the old Water Tower, one of the few downtown buildings to have survived the Great Chicago Fire of 1871, then on by Orchestra Hall and the Art Institute. If she wanted more exercise, she continued on down State Street to Marshall Field's with its lovely Tiffany dome, and Carson Pirie Scott's spectacular store. "I grew up in a small town. City architecture is fascinating to me—I feel like a little girl ogling the tall buildings. And I can window-shop for hours, but I rarely buy." She laughed at herself, then realized Chris hadn't said a word in a long time. "What museums do you like best?" she asked.

"Oh, well it's so hard to choose," Chris said quickly, glancing up at the professor for the first time in ages. "I mean, I like them all, of course."

"But you must have your favorite," she insisted enthusiastically, sure that their tastes would mesh. "Wait, let me guess. I bet you like the Museum of Science and Industry. Guys are always into that sort of thing."

Chris seemed increasingly restless. He kept shifting in his seat, glancing at the instructor and scribbling out sporadic notes. She felt badly for taking his mind off the lecture; he obviously was interested in it.

"Actually," he murmured. "My favorite is the Art Institute. I go there a lot."

She grinned at him as the lights came up in the auditorium. "That's my favorite, too! We should visit together some afternoon when you're free."

"Great," he said, absently jotting down a few final words. "We'll do that."

She was about to ask him if later that same day would be okay, when Kraig raised his voice to reach the very back rows.

"Your projects will be due following midterms. I'll let you know the exact date once we see how you're progressing," he said. "Remember, you'll need to sign up with a friend, since two people are required for each team. It will be easiest if you pair up with someone in your Wednesday/Friday classes."

Chris scowled and Madelyn felt the bottom drop out of her stomach. "What was that all about?" she gasped.

The boy who'd shushed them turned around and said with a sneer, "If you guys had been listening instead of flirting, you'd know."

Chris rolled his eyes as he watched their classmate pick up his books and move down the row of seats. "Drip," he muttered halfheartedly.

Madelyn moved over closer to him and peered over his arm at the scanty notes on his paper.

"We have to choose two poets from a list posted outside Kraig's office. Using samples of their work, we contrast their styles."

"Why do we work in teams?" Madelyn asked, embarrassed that she hadn't been listening closer.

"Each partner studies one poet and analyzes him or her. Then the two partners pool their notes and write up the paper together. After we're done, we switch poets, then see if we've changed our minds about the outcome of the paper."

"We? You mean...you and me?"

"I thought I'd sign us up together, if that's okay with you," he said.

Madelyn smiled at him, pleased that they'd have a built-in excuse to spend time together. "Fine with me," she said breezily.

"Good. When's your next class?" Chris asked, an intriguing look in his eyes.

"I have one now, across campus," she explained. He was standing so close to her and talking in that husky male voice that let her know he was thinking about *her,* not school any longer. "Then," she continued slowly, "I have two more later in the afternoon. What about you?"

"No more today. Mine are sort of lopsided. A lot on Tuesdays and Thursdays, and I have a couple of labs on Saturdays," he added quickly. "But I didn't really want to go back across town to my apartment just yet."

"If you need a place to study for a while, you can come back with me to the dorm," she suggested, feeling drunk with her new confidence. She hoped Sandy would be there to see Chris. Or maybe it would be better if she weren't there. Madelyn didn't want her curvaceous blond roomie flirting with him. "I mean, well, you could stay there and I'd see you after my other morning class."

"I have a better idea," Chris said, slipping the fingers of his right hand between hers and drawing her still closer.

"Why don't we take a picnic lunch out on the Plaisance and start planning our project?"

The mischievous twinkle in his eye let her know again that scholastic pursuits weren't the only thing on his mind.

"Okay," she said, playing along. "There's some bologna, bread and fruit in my fridge. You can make us sandwiches while I go to my next class."

"I'll pick you up after your class. Where is it?" he asked.

"Murphy Hall."

He grinned at her. "I'll be there."

Sandy wasn't in the room when they arrived there, and Madelyn felt odd leaving Chris alone in her room. But he assured her that he'd make out just fine.

All through her sociology lecture, Madelyn couldn't stop thinking about Chris. Before leaving the dorm, she'd gone to the ladies' room and discovered that her period had started. A wave of the usual subtle weakness and vulnerability came with it. But she also felt happier and more at one with herself than she had in days. She couldn't believe she'd just told a hunk like Chris to make himself at home in her room and pack sandwiches for their lunch. She couldn't believe the happy turn her life had taken.

Chris felt strange hanging out in Madelyn's room while she was in class, but it was a nice kind of strange. He liked the smell of the tiny room, reminiscent of a flower shop. He liked how everything had its place, from the bottles of perfume on the shelf above her bed to the orderly rows of texts and reference books lined up on her desk between marble bookends shaped like the lions outside the New York Public Library.

When he left, having finished packing their meal and found a stadium blanket beneath her bed, he got curious looks from some of the girls on the floor and guessed Mad-

elyn would have plenty of questions to answer later. She was so shy, he wondered if that would bother her.

Chris strolled across the university grounds, soaking up the cultured essence of the place. Everything seemed so refined here, so bound in history and tradition. It made him feel as if he were an important part of something very big and long lasting—a feeling he'd never had as a kid. Maybe this institution would one day take the place of a family for him.

Chris paced up and down in front of the main entrance of the soaring, gray nouveau-Gothic Murphy Hall. He waited ten minutes beneath a gnarled oak before Madelyn stepped through the granite arch. His heart leapt in his chest, and his mouth suddenly felt dry with desire. One kiss from Madelyn had excited him more than he could have believed possible.

But he had to squelch his desire to rush up to her, pull her into his arms and crush her lips beneath his.

"Hungry?" he asked, trying to sound casual.

"Famished," she admitted, beaming at him.

He took her hand in his and led her toward the Plaisance. It had been the midway for the World's Columbian Exposition in 1893, before Rockefeller had established the university on the same site. There were plenty of benches in the parklike setting, amidst graceful trees and carefully tended flower beds brimming with vivid yellow and rusty red mums.

"Let's not eat on the Plaisance," Madelyn said, breathlessly.

"Why not?" Chris asked, afraid that she'd changed her mind and would pick a less private place, such as the student center.

"I have a better idea. We can walk across Hyde Park to the Japanese garden. It's beautiful this time of year, and

there are plenty of shady spots to spread out a blanket—since you thought of one."

Chris grinned. "Great!"

There were also plenty of intimate niches tucked among the fall foliage, which would screen them from passersby. Again the thought of their kiss ran a chill up his spine, and he felt as light-headed as a little boy does when his dad surprises him with tickets to a baseball game. He felt drunk with the promise of being alone, *really* alone with Madelyn.

Their first kiss had been a light appetizer; he wanted the four-course meal.

But he reminded himself of his pledge to her. He'd have to go slow, consider her feelings and make very sure that he didn't press her to do anything she didn't feel comfortable with.

"The Japanese garden sounds fine," he said, hoping she couldn't hear his heart whamming away in his chest.

They strolled across the campus, at last crossing Cornell Drive with its rush of traffic and into Jackson Park where the garden was located within sight of the Museum of Science and Industry. A generous September sun shone down on them, and Chris felt almost too warm in his leather jacket. He stopped to take it off and sling it over one arm before continuing.

"You pick the spot," he said, eyeing an inviting clearing within a cluster of Oriental shrubbery.

Madelyn followed his gaze and smiled. "Looks good to me. We can see the fountains from there."

Chris didn't know about seeing any fountains, but he liked the secluded atmosphere. A ripple of anticipation slithered through his groin.

Slow down, boy. Slow down! he cautioned himself.

Madelyn rested her knapsack in the grass, then pulled the thin blanket out of the bag Chris carried. He watched her,

enjoying the grace of her simple movements as she shook out the red plaid blanket then let it settle in a tartan cloud across the thin browning grass. Her pert breasts moved tantalizingly beneath the fabric of her lightweight jacket. He was glad he hadn't waited until December to meet her, when the ground would be covered with snow and ice and she would be buried under layers of sweaters and a parka.

Snapping out of his reverie, Chris caught two corners of the blanket and helped her straighten it. Then he sat down and started pulling out sandwiches, two pears, a small bag of sour-cream-and-onion potato chips, which he'd brought from home that morning for emergency munchies and two cans of soda he'd bought from a machine on the way over to meet Madelyn.

"This is a feast!" she cried, her eyes lighting up with delight.

She's beautiful! he thought, enthralled with her. When they'd first met, she'd seemed pretty to him in a different sort of way. Her turned-up nose, clear brown eyes and lovely skin were particularly remarkable when considered separately. But together, in the golden light of an autumn afternoon, they grabbed him by the throat and left him breathless.

He sat limply on the blanket, ignoring his food and books for the moment, content to study her.

"Aren't you hungry?" she asked, smiling softly at him as she bit into her sandwich.

"Oh...oh, sure. I am."

Recovering with some effort, he reached for the other sandwich. But he ate slowly, unable to take his eyes from her mouth as her lips moved to nibble daintily at the triangles of bread and bologna.

"This is good," he said between bites.

"Mmmm," she agreed through a full mouth. "My mom used to make me bologna-and-mustard sandwiches every day for school lunch."

He laughed. "You must have gotten sick of them."

"No," she replied solemnly. "I'm allergic to peanuts, so I couldn't eat peanut butter and jelly like my friends. Bologna was my favorite."

"No peanut butter! You poor deprived child!"

He reached out to jokingly pat her on the head, but found that his hand sought out her cheek instead. Slowly he stroked the velvety swell over her cheekbone, then traveled across her jawline, down her long silky throat. He traced the gentle hollow at the base of her throat with one fingertip. The V of her button-down oxford blouse beckoned his hand farther downward....

She didn't tell him to stop or slap his hand away, but instead interrupted its descent with a shaky question. "Don't you think we should start choosing poets while we eat?"

Chris forced himself to withdraw his hand. "I guess," he said, sighing.

"Unless you'd rather wait...until we've finished eating," she said diplomatically. "Whatever you want."

At that moment the only thing he wanted was to press Madelyn down on the stadium blanket in the middle of the garden and make beautiful love with her.

"No, we can start working," he said quietly.

She nodded and reached for a thick, black library book she'd asked him to bring from her room. As she stretched across the blanket for *Favorite Poets of the World*, her blouse gaped above the top pearl button, and the swell of her left breast showed beneath the cotton poplin.

Chris involuntarily drew a sharp breath, unable to drag his eyes off the smooth, pink mound. Heat rushed through his groin as he envisioned her naked. Her breasts weren't flat, as her slight figure might have suggested, only petite

and in excellent proportion with her small hips and tiny waist. He became vividly aware of his size and strength, sensing that it would take nothing for him to press her back onto the soft wool and slip his hand beneath her skirt and tantalize her until she asked—no, *begged*—him to satisfy her.

But he knew he couldn't force himself on her. She was too precious for that caveman treatment.

Chris reached toward the book in her hand, locking his eyes with hers. He gently touched the back of her hand. "I already took a look through there, back at the dorm while you were in class," he said softly.

"Oh, good. Do you know who you want for your poet?" she asked.

He wished he could tell what she was thinking. She looked perfectly relaxed, yet her breathing seemed a little fast, as if she were as excited as he was by their closeness.

He nodded slowly, keeping her eyes captive in his glance. "'The fountains mingle with the river, / And the rivers with the ocean; / The winds of heaven mix for ever, / With a sweet emotion; / Nothing in the world is single...'" He reached up to touch her lips with one finger. "'All things, by a law divine, / In one another's being mingle. / Why not I with thine?'"

She gazed at him in rapt fascination, her lower lip quivering under his touch. "Do you know the rest?" she whispered hoarsely.

Chris inched over closer on his hip, tracing her pink mouth with the guitar-string callused index finger of his left hand. "'See! the mountains kiss high heaven, / And the waves clasp one another; / No sister flower would be forgiven if it disdained its brother; / And the sunlight clasps the earth, / And the moonbeams kiss the sea...'" He drew a deep breath and lengthened his lean body to bring his lips

within a heartbeat of hers. "'What are all these kissings worth, / If thou kiss not me?'"

For an endless moment, Madelyn gazed at him with tears clinging to her long lashes. "Shelley," she murmured. "You know Shelley's poems. How beautiful."

Then she leaned toward him, closing the space between them until their lips softly touched. His hand came up behind her neck, coaxing her to linger in their kiss. Again, her mouth parted tentatively, and this time he took advantage of her willingness. He deepened their kiss, savoring her, letting her taste him. Fire roared through his body, centering erotically within his male essence. Chris let out a soft moan.

Madelyn pulled gently away, but only by a few inches.

Her face glowed with passion. He had been ready to apologize immediately, if she'd shown the least sign of distaste at their kiss, or at his reaction to it. Now he could see with relief that that wouldn't be necessary.

"You smell wonderful," he growled from deep down in his throat. "You taste like—"

She placed her fingertips over his mouth and smiled shyly. "I liked it, too. And I loved the Shelley. But maybe," she suggested without a trace of coyness, "maybe we should get to work... and take the rest a step at a time?"

He took a restorative breath, settled his hormones as well as they could be settled and nodded in agreement. "Sure." Then he winked at her. "You're right. Time for that later. And," he added firmly, "there *will* be a time... the *right* time."

"I know," she said, smiling.

Seven

Chris had never felt happier. Everything had always come hard for him, or not at all. Madelyn was the sweetest, easiest joy he'd ever known. For once, something was going right in his life.

They spent Tuesday afternoon, after the classes he'd made up for her benefit, reading snatches of love poems to each other. He read more of Percy Bysshe Shelley's works to her—flowery with old-fashioned romanticism. She read McKuen selections to him—gutsy, modern, twentieth century and rough with emotion.

Madelyn never flinched at the words of passion, and he loved knowing that he was probably the only person to whom this shy girl could have possibly read such intimate lines.

On Wednesday they met again—this time in her room at the dorm. They ended up reading very little but making out a great deal on top of her bed.

"Oh, stop! Stop! Enough!" Chris groaned, stretching out on the soft pink comforter, pretending he was exhausted after their playful kissing. He closed his eyes, enjoying the warmth of her closeness. He could feel her hovering over him, and he reached up to sandwich her head between his palms.

When he opened his eyes, her lovely, oval face looked down on him, but there was suddenly a frightened look in her eyes that he hadn't seen before. He released her quickly, leaving it to her to be the aggressor. Her eyes were wide,

dark and full of unanswered questions. But she bravely leaned down and kissed him on the mouth, then darted her tongue between his teeth and came away gasping for air with a pretty flush to her cheeks.

To his surprise, she took his hand between hers.

"Touch me," she whispered, placing his fingers on the front of her blouse. She closed her eyes as if intent on absorbing the warmth of his touch. The contours of her face began to relax as she pressed his hand against her breast.

At first, he didn't dare do anything more than softly caress her through the fabric; then he slowly moved his hand between the buttons. Something in the tension of her body told him she still wasn't ready for all he had in mind. He figured she wasn't a virgin, but she probably hadn't been with many guys, and maybe there had been no one for a long time.

Take it easy, McGuire, a voice warned him. *Don't scare her off.*

He gently cupped her left breast and let it warm his palm. Cautiously, he ran his fingertips over and around the taut nipple. He laid his head on the other breast and, with a supreme effort, withdrew his hand....

Chris woke up Thursday morning with a hard-on. He rolled over in bed, pressing his fists between his thighs with a groan. The image in his mind of Madelyn was so sensually vivid, he could almost feel her breasts cupped within his palms and hear her soft, pleading sighs. He came almost immediately.

Unable to go back to sleep, he shot up out of bed. It was still dark, only 6:00 a.m., but he had a plan in mind.

After a quick wash-up, Chris pulled on his most comfortable outfit—a tattered pair of jeans and stretched-out sweatshirt with the Grateful Dead skull on the front. Ex-

GETTING REAL: CHRISTOPHER 91

ploding through his apartment door, he raced across the hall and pounded on the girls' door.

"Who the hell is it?" shrieked someone from the other side.

He grinned, recognizing Becky's voice, although her choice of wording was uncharacteristic for the elfin girl from rural Illinois.

"It's Chris! I got an emergency—let me in!"

Immediately, the door flew open, and Becky stood in her nightshirt, wearing a worried expression. "You all right? What happened?"

"Nothing yet...." Well, that wasn't the precise truth, but as close as he was going to get. "I need you guys to help me."

"At six in the morning?" Jessica called out. Apparently she'd been listening from her bedroom. He could hear her rousting C.J. out of bed.

"Like I said, it's an emergency, and I know you guys all have to go to work today, so I had to catch you early."

C.J. plodded into the living room, wearing footed flannel pajamas and clutching an enormous stuffed bear. She looked remarkably like a little kid woken from a sound sleep. With a loud groan, she collapsed into the tattered armchair across from the couch where Becky and Chris sat.

Jessica perched demurely on the chair arm and glared at him. "This had better be damn good, buster."

Chris swallowed. "Hey, don't get all bent out of shape. I really need you guys." He took a deep breath, trying to organize his thoughts. "You know that girl I was telling you about?" Chris asked.

"Madelyn...in your English class," Jessica said.

"Right. Well, everything's going great with her." He looked at each of them in succession. "And I mean, *everything*. She's smart, pretty, warm, has a super sense of humor...and, well..."

"She wants your body. So what else is new?" Jessica spouted tartly.

"No, it's not like that at all. She's different from the other girls. If you met her, you'd know that."

Becky considered him doubtfully. "Go on."

"Yeah... anyway, we've gotten pretty friendly in the last week. It's happening faster than I'd hoped for."

"Which is bad?" C.J. asked.

"No, of course it's good. But we meet in the Japanese garden on campus, or in her dorm. And there's no way I'm going to sleep with her in her room with girls running up and down the hall at all hours, or in some cheap motel room." He struggled to come up with the words he needed. "If we make love—and it's beginning to look like that's inevitable—I want her to feel special. I want to make her really comfortable with the place. I don't want her to get the idea she's just one in a long line of—"

"Sluts?" Jessica put in with an innocent smile.

"Hey, the girls I've dated aren't tramps," Chris defended his ex's.

Becky lowered her eyes. "Well, you have to admit, Chris, none of them have lasted very long. Maybe they were interested in the same thing you were—just the physical part of a relationship. Maybe that's why you sought each other out."

"I suppose," he groaned, lowering his head into his hands.

"But now there's Madelyn," C.J. said, bringing them back to the point at hand.

He sat up straight again, the warm feeling her name summoned filling his veins. "Yeah. And she's different from all the others. She's like... like a streak of gold in the middle of granite."

"How poetic," Jessica teased.

He felt his face heat up and wondered if he was actually blushing. "As a matter of fact, we've been studying poetry together when we haven't been doing other things. But the point is, I want to start bringing her over to my place."

All three girls' faces froze in expressions of horror.

"My God, you can't do that!" C.J. gasped. "That apartment is a disaster zone!"

Jessica nodded firmly. "The health department should have condemned it months ago. Last time I set foot in the place, I found orange peels on the coffee table that looked like they'd been there since last Christmas."

"Easter," he admitted guiltily.

"There are dirty dishes everywhere and wall-to-wall dirty clothes," C.J. said.

"I did my laundry."

"Well, that leaves only about a foot-deep layer of clutter to wade through," Becky commented. "Madelyn ought to be really impressed."

Chris shot her a nasty look.

"Nothing personal, Chris," Becky said gently. "You just make a lousy housekeeper... worse than Jessica."

The willowy blonde scrunched up her nose at her roommate.

"That's why I need you three to help me out," Chris cried.

Jessica shot to her feet. "Whoa. I'm not cleaning your apartment. That's where I draw the line in a friendship."

Becky nodded. "She's right. Keeping our own place is tough enough."

Chris turned pleadingly to C.J. Even this generous girl who'd acted as if she'd do anything for him, looked skeptical.

"It would take a bulldozer and a five-man janitorial squad to make a dent on that place. There's not much I could do on my own," she said apologetically. She looked

at the other two girls. "But maybe we could just go over and sort of give Chris some advice on what *he* should do first?"

Jessica rolled her eyes. "C.J., if you think that getting us over there will make any difference—"

"Let's walk through with Chris and survey the damage. It's only a little after six. I don't have to be at the TV station until noon today, since we're shooting a special promo for the weather show."

"Yeah, but Becky and I still have to be at work by nine at the latest," Jessica added.

"Then we've all got at least a couple of hours to help Chris get the work organized," C.J. suggested tactfully. She winked at him conspiratorially.

Jessica groaned. "All right. Let's get this over with."

"Yes!" Chris shouted, thrusting a fist triumphantly in the air as he leapt out off the couch. He dimmed his enthusiasm at a cold glance from Jessica.

It took only five minutes for the girls to sum up the situation.

"This is an interior decorator's hell," Jessica stated.

She crossed her arms over her chest as she scowled, first at the mountain of dirty dishes rising out of the sink, then the pile of beer and soda cans that had tumbled down from a pyramid constructed at Chris's last party.

"Wait," Becky said, tapping her finger thoughtfully on her chin. "The key is not to look at the apartment as a whole, but separate it into separate jobs. Look, Chris, if you go around with a garbage bag and throw out the empties, used paper plates and cups and empty the ashtrays, you'll at least be able to see the dirt."

"And what you can see, you can clean!" C.J. added. "It's really more clutter than dirt anyway."

Chris was already lunging for the cupboard under the sink. He straightened up with box of plastic trash bags in

one hand. "The magic ingredient!" he exclaimed, holding them aloft.

He took a bag and started in on the kitchen. C.J. and Becky looked at each other and picked up bags. With a grumble, Jessica started going through Chris's mail that was piled on the kitchen counter. She threw out most of it, but found two unpaid phone bills and a notice from the student-aid office that hadn't been opened. She handed them to Chris with a stern look.

"Thanks," he said meekly.

Chris moved on, trash bag in hand, to the bathroom and then to the bedroom area. He scooped two empty Oreo bags and a Pringles tube from under the bed before returning to the living room.

"There," C.J. said, her hands on her wide hips as she surveyed the apartment. Six bags of trash had been cleared away. "It doesn't look so bad."

Chris scowled. Now that the mess had been disposed of, he could see dust motes tumbling when anyone moved. Cobwebs clung to the corners of the ceiling, and the kitchen countertops were spattered with grease.

"Sure, looks great! Nothing a few minutes with a blowtorch couldn't fix," he muttered.

"There *is* an inch of soap scum in the shower stall," Becky pointed out. "And—" she ran the toe of her slipper across the living room carpet "—I'm not sure what color this rug was."

"Green," Chris said.

C.J. waved off her friends' complaints. "Chris, go down to the Food Fair and rent one of those industrial-strength carpet shampooers. I'll vacuum while you're gone. Oh, and buy about a gallon of carpet-cleaning solution—the concentrated kind." She pushed him out the door. As he closed it behind him, he heard the girls fighting over who was going to get stuck with scrubbing his bathroom.

He could have kissed all three of them.

Chris knew he couldn't see Madelyn until that night. He'd told her that he had classes until five—just in case Jimmy called to set up a practice. But he didn't hear from him all day, and he began to wonder if his old friend had decided to make a go of the band without him.

Chris met Madelyn at the dorm at seven o'clock.

Her door was open, and he knocked on the jamb.

"Come in!" two voices chorused.

Madelyn smiled at him as he walked in. The girl with her was tall and well built; she could have been a model. She was the kind he'd sought out since he was in high school. Cheerleader material. A babe. But now she just looked like all the rest. Beautiful, but ordinary in other ways beside his Madelyn.

He smiled politely. "You must be Sandy."

"Right!" There was a surprised twinkle in her eyes, and he caught her flashing a look of approval toward Madelyn—a girl's version of the male checkout. "Hi, Chris. I've heard a lot about you."

"Oh?" He grinned at Madelyn, and was rewarded with a blush.

"I told her about the project," Madelyn said quickly. She straightened up, trying to look businesslike. He noticed she wore a skirt tonight, which happened to be a good two inches shorter than her usual dresses. The soft, pastel pleats flattered her slim legs. A fuzzy pink sweater topped off the outfit. It fit perfectly, outlining the gentle swell of her breasts. Suddenly his jeans felt much too tight.

"You guys can work here, if you like," Sandy said briskly, gathering up books, a notebook and her purse. "I was on my way out."

Madelyn shot her a grateful smile.

"That's okay. Stay," Chris said. "I thought we might work somewhere else."

Madelyn looked disappointed. "The lounge? But I heard there was going to be some kind of meeting down there... it'll be hard to concentrate, and the library is always so crowded...."

The words bubbled out of her. He had trouble keeping a straight face. She obviously wanted privacy as much as he did, and that knowledge drove him up a wall. He couldn't wait to be alone with her, to touch her, to reach beyond the gently exploring kisses and caresses they'd shared.

"Not there," he said casually. "I was thinking of my place. We can take the Jeffrey almost to my doorstep."

Madelyn hesitated.

"Well, since you're not staying, maybe I'll just settle in for the night," Sandy said, dropping her books on the bed with emphasis. She cast Chris a look that said, "Sometimes you gotta give her a push."

"Oh," Madelyn said, then smiled hesitantly, "well, I guess that's okay. I'll just get my things together, and..." She riffled through her top bureau drawer, slipping something discreetly into her roomy leather purse, then shoved in a couple of pens and a pocket notebook, as well. "There, ready."

The bus came almost as soon as they'd arrived at the 57th Street stop. They sat in silence, holding hands as the bus grumbled its way across Hyde Park to 47th Street then cut north along Lake Shore Drive. The moon cast an orange glow over the surface of Lake Michigan and reflected off the dark windows of the surrounding buildings.

When they arrived in front of his apartment building, Chris looked up at it with mixed emotions. The Loop had plenty of posh addresses, with expensive price tags. His building looked a little squalid beside the others.

"This is home," he said simply. "Not much, but it's cheap and I have great neighbors."

She smiled. "I think it's nice, Chris. I'd like to live off-campus someday, too."

A warm feeling closed around his heart. Was she hinting that she might consider moving in with him someday? Having her lie with him in bed even once seemed almost too much to hope for. Waking up to her sweet face every morning would be heaven!

Reining in his excitement, he led her to the elevator, which miraculously happened to be working that night.

"Why did you pick the Loop to live in?" she asked as they rode up. "It's so far off-campus."

He couldn't tell her the real reasons he'd picked it.

"I wanted to live in the real world. You know, not get totally sucked into campus life."

She smiled at him. "That must be the artist in you talking."

"The artist?" The word conjured up a picture of him poised before an easel, a brush in hand.

"You know, your guitar. You're a classical musician."

"Oh, that," he mumbled, then quickly escorted her off the elevator and down the corridor.

He wondered fleetingly if the girls were in. He could almost imagine C.J. posted at the peephole in their door, signaling to her roommates and whispering, "She's here! She's here! Come take a look!"

He grinned at the thought.

"What's that for?" Madelyn asked as he turned the key in the lock.

"What?"

"That weird smile."

"Nothing," he said quickly. "Come on in so we can... um, can get to work."

He let Madelyn go in first and held his breath while she stood in the living room, surveying the newly shampooed carpet, the scuffed fourth-hand kitchenette set Jessica had lemon-oiled, the worn but thoroughly vacuumed couch and the bowl of fruit that Becky had thoughtfully arranged on the narrow stretch of countertop between the living room and kitchen areas.

"This is really nice, Chris," Madelyn breathed, her lips lifting with approval as she put her purse and books down on the counter and took off her jacket. "Most single guys have no idea how to keep a decent home."

"Really?" he choked out, trying to keep a straight face.

"No, I'm serious. They're such pigs. I love your place. It's sort of Spartan, but that's just right for a guy, and it makes the space seem bigger anyway."

"It is pretty small. Not much bigger than a closet."

She looked at the single set of drawers, the bedside table and the double bed with its freshly laundered navy blue cord bedspread.

He came up behind her and wrapped his arms around her tiny waist, nestling his chin in the silky strands of her hair. "I did a little tidying up before you came," he confessed in a low voice.

He could feel her heartbeat through the wall of his chest as she rested back against him.

"That was thoughtful of you," she whispered.

He was potently aware of her small, tight bottom curving into the hollow of his groin. She felt warm and inviting, and he wondered if she were as aware of the hardness of his body in contrast to the softness of hers.

Chris stepped back quickly, not wanting her to think that sex was the reason he'd brought her here... although the thought of her sprawled naked on his bed was an image he'd enjoyed frequently throughout the week.

As soon as they parted, she spun around and stepped into his embrace, tossing her arms up around his neck and pressing her head on his chest with a deep sigh. "Oh, Chris, this is so much *nicer* than the old dorm. Thank you!"

"You're welcome," he said, unsure whether she meant his apartment was a clean, quiet place to study, or that it would provide the intimacy she, too, had longed for.

She snuggled for a long moment within his arms. His heart raced, and his body sizzled as she melted into him.

"Chris," she murmured at last, "can I ask you a question?"

"S-sure," he forced out, hardly able to breathe any longer. He wished he could see her face to help him puzzle out what she was thinking.

"Why haven't you tried to make love to me?"

"What?" The word exploded from his lips.

"Why haven't you—"

"I heard... I just wasn't sure..." Chris squeezed Madelyn, kissing the top of her head, then drew a fortifying breath. "I've wanted to make love to you from the first moment I saw you," he whispered.

She audibly swallowed. "But there have been other girls—lots of girls before me," she said tightly. "Haven't there?"

"Yes," he admitted.

"And you waited this long with each of them?"

"It's not so long. We've only known each other a few weeks."

"It seems like forever," she murmured.

"I know."

"Oh, dammit, Chris!" She pushed away from him with an impatient, angry little-girl jerk and stomped across the living room. "What's wrong with me?"

Chris was completely at a loss. He followed her into the living room but stood a little apart from her. Fury had

turned her brown eyes into smoldering coals. He felt he'd be wise to give her space.

"Wrong with you? There's *nothing* wrong with you," he sputtered.

She lunged for her purse, unzipped it and pulled out a pink vinyl cosmetic bag. From between tubes of lipstick and mascara, she pulled a tiny, foil-wrapped object.

"A condom?" He laughed out loud.

"Yes. I was sure you'd *do* something. You acted as if you were attracted to me. You kissed me like...like..." She suddenly seemed short of breath, and tears welled up in her eyes, spoiling her indignant female act.

He smiled at her and stepped forward, gently removing the packet from her upraised fingertips. "I kissed you as if I wanted to make love to you?"

She nodded, her lips pressed together. She was trying desperately not to cry, and the effort was more appealing to him than she could ever know.

Chris slipped the condom into his back jeans pocket, alongside the one he'd been carrying around since Wednesday a week ago when he'd set out to search for her in English class. He reached out, grabbed her shoulders and pulled her into him.

"I've never wanted a woman more than I've wanted you, Madelyn. And I want to make love to you now. But I..." It was so difficult to explain. "See, I haven't done much right in my life."

She started to speak, and he shut her up with a gentle brush of his lips over hers.

"No, listen to me. I've made a lot of mistakes, and stuff hasn't worked out for me...until now. You are the best thing in my life. I didn't want to blow it by being a jerk and jumping your bones the first time we were alone together!"

"Oh," she murmured, but her voice held a pleased note.

"Some things are worth doing right," he said softly. "I figured, with you, that meant taking it slow. Waiting until we were both ready. When it felt right to both of us, we'd make love."

She took a long moment to digest his words. "Does it feel right to you tonight?" she asked bashfully.

"Yes," he said, drawing his hand upward to caress the side of her breast through her blouse. "It feels very right to me. What about you?"

"I... Oh, Chris... please make love to me," she whispered.

He'd never heard more beautiful words.

Nothing in the world, not his fights with Jimmy about the band, not his dad's wasted life, not his own confused wanderings across the country made a bit of difference. All that mattered to him was Madelyn, and the realization that she was here, in his arms, because there was nowhere else on earth that she'd rather be at this moment in time.

The other girls, the other times, seemed to be part of another lifetime. He gazed down into her beautiful face and marveled at the delicate shape of her cheekbones, the quiver along her perfect lips and the shimmer in her eyes. She was blinking back the tears—tears of joy, he now realized.

Hungrily, Chris lowered his mouth over hers. Every instinct in his body ached to fling her little body to the floor and press himself on top of her, into her. He wanted her *now*, hard and fast!

But he reined himself in and settled for deepening their kiss, combing his fingers through the long brown strands of her hair as he framed and held her pretty face between his hands. She returned his fevered kiss with a vengeance, drinking of him as if she'd been thirsty all of her young life.

"Oh, Chris!" she gasped when their mouths finally parted.

He smiled, pleased at her reaction. Before tonight, he'd been afraid of breaking her if he breathed too hard on her. But she'd seemed to enjoy the intensity of their embrace.

With trembling hands, he slipped the little pearl buttons through the holes in the front of her neatly pressed cotton blouse. He gently divided the embroidered collar, revealing her collar bones, and the tempting hollow at their juncture. Leaning forward, he traced his tongue around the soft valley. She dropped her head back and shivered as his mouth worked magic on her. Chris unbuttoned two more of the tiny circles and spread the fabric wider. The delicate swell of her breasts rose above the white lace cups of her bra. Breathing hard, he slipped his right hand beneath the pretty silk and cupped her breast in one hand. A jagged flash of heat raced through his loins. He enjoyed the sensation, prolonging it by rubbing the pad of his thumb back and forth over Madelyn's tiny, brown nipple, watching it come erect under his ministrations.

She seemed terribly quiet. Although her body was responding to him, he felt the need to be sure that she wanted this as much as he did. In five more minutes, he'd have one hell of a time turning back.

"Are you all right?" he rasped out.

"Oh," she moaned softly. "This feels wonderful...."

He smiled. Guess that was still a go.

He bent and, lifting her breast above the undergarment, drew his tongue lightly over her nipple. She stiffened. He covered her breast with his mouth and drew it into his mouth, sucking gently, loving the way she squirmed with pleasure in his arms while gasping lightly.

Slipping his hand down farther and inside the elasticized band of her skirt, he caressed the butter-soft flesh of her stomach and reached slowly inside her panties. His fingers slid through the soft fur of her feminine mound and, at last,

reached the hot, liquid center of her womanhood. He could contain himself no longer.

Lifting her in his arms, he carried her to his bed. Gently he laid her on top of the spread. Her prim skirt and blouse, ordinarily flawlessly smooth, were a rumpled mess, and she looked incredibly wanton to him.

His eyes never left hers as he pulled his shirt up over his head, then unbuckled his belt, unzipped his jeans and pulled them down over his lean hips. She watched him unabashedly, drinking in every line of his body. When he pulled off his briefs, she looked at him, then snapped her head away with a strangled gasp.

"What's wrong?" he demanded a little put out as he stared down at himself. He thought he looked pretty damn impressive.

"Nothing," she choked out, focusing on his eyes as if she didn't dare look lower again. "I just..."

"You just what?"

As he stretched out beside her on the bed, she timidly reached down and enclosed him in her hand. "Oh, my!" she breathed. "You're wonderful."

He threw his head back and laughed at her. "You're sure easy to please. All I have to do is get a hard-on?"

"Maybe it's the...anticipation?" she murmured from down deep in her throat.

Then he knew it was time. He moved on top of her and unwrapped the foil package she'd given him before. Gently nudging apart her long legs, he entered her smoothly and brought her to ecstasy and her first orgasm before he allowed himself to join her in a whirl of heat and passion that lasted far into the night.

Eight

Madelyn's slim, silky body draped across Chris's chest, her cheek nestling on his bare shoulder, her eyes closed. He couldn't tell if she was really sleeping or simply floating in the sublime aftermath of their lovemaking.

He was lost in his own bliss. Although he'd imagined making love with her time and again, the act itself had far surpassed any flight of his mind. She was softer, sweeter, more honestly responsive to his touch than any woman he'd ever known.

As if coming from a great distance, an irritating sound interfered with the gentle mesh of his and Madelyn's breathing. For a moment, he couldn't isolate it; then it dawned on him that someone was knocking on his front door.

Chris started to extricate himself from Madelyn's arms to go to the door, then decided he didn't want to leave the warm bed and Madelyn's warmer body.

"Go away!" he shouted after a second knock.

He'd thought his visitor had left when a voice shouted through the door. "Hey, Chris! It's me, C.J.!"

"For crying out loud," he grumbled under his breath.

"Just wanted to bring you a cheesecake," his too-neighborly neighbor went on blithely, although he hadn't answered her. "I thought you two might—"

He could hear a second voice. Apparently someone had come along and was talking to the generous, but pesty girl.

"Chris," C.J. continued in a more subdued tone, "I'll just leave it out here in the hall. You can get it anytime you like."

"Thanks," he called out, grinning at the ceiling. Good old Jessica must have read C.J. the riot act and dragged her back inside their apartment.

"Who was that?" Madelyn murmured drowsily.

"One of the three girls who live across the hall. C.J. seems to think I'm underfed. She's always baking stuff for me."

"That's nice." Madelyn sighed.

He moved his hand over her naked hip, enjoying the satiny feel of her flesh beneath his palm.

"Are you going to sleep?" he asked, continuing to stroke her.

She stretched and purred, catlike. "No. I'm just feeling mellow." Opening one eye, she squinted at him. "Play for me."

"What?"

"Play for me... the guitar. I want to hear what you're working on." She sat up in bed, adjusting the sheets to cover her breasts and gazing at him with innocent curiosity.

"I... But I don't have anything special prepared," he stammered.

"I don't care. Just play something simple and sweet. It doesn't have to be flamenco, although I'm wild about it. It's such sexy music, don't you think?" In her excitement, the sheets fell in folds around her waist. "A baroque piece maybe."

He couldn't very well refuse to play for Madelyn. But he didn't want to think what her reaction would be if he plugged in his amps and broke out in wild feedback vibes, a prelude to the number his band had last rehearsed. Then he remembered his old acoustic guitar, collecting dust in the coat closet.

"Okay," he said, "but stay here. I want to play for you in bed."

She grinned at him, her brown eyes sparkling as brightly as if he'd just given her a priceless jewel.

Bounding out of bed, Chris grabbed a towel from the bathroom and wrapped it around his hips. He didn't want it for the sake of modesty; he needed it to tidy up the guitar.

After he'd finished dusting off the instrument, he rewrapped himself and joined Madelyn, sitting Indian-style in a nest of mussed bedclothes.

"It's beautiful," she breathed, touching the sleek wood of the guitar's body.

"I bought it from a secondhand shop when I was in tenth grade. It was never a very expensive guitar, but it had a nice sound," he murmured, running his fingers fondly over the strings. He fretted and plucked one string at a time, tightening or loosening it with the screw on the neck.

At last Chris had tuned it to his satisfaction. He tried out a few runs, then set to recalling one of the few pieces of Bach he'd learned.

Back when he was in New York, trying to scrape by while he searched for connections to get him into a decent band, he'd bussed dishes at some dive on 49th Street. While he was there he met a guy who taught guitar. Roy also had a Harley that needed some work done on it. Chris had once had a bike and had worked on it himself, so he'd agreed to repair Roy's motorcycle in exchange for three hours of lessons.

He hadn't realized until he'd arrived at Roy's apartment that his instructor was into classical guitar and hadn't a clue about modern rock, jazz, rockabilly or any of the other varieties Chris might have been interested in. So, in spite of himself, he'd learned some Bach, and he'd surprised himself by liking it.

He couldn't remember the names of many of the pieces—one had originally been a violin sonata in G minor, complete with sustained chord tones and double-stops—but he recalled the feel of the gut strings vibrating beneath his fingers and the gentle tones that seemed to flow like a clear, woodsy stream from the instrument.

Now, sitting beside Madelyn on his bed, he curled his body around the guitar, closed his eyes in concentration and played the sweet, rolling notes. He played for ten minutes, nearly exhausting his limited repertoire, before Madelyn breathed a word.

"That's beautiful," she whispered, when he'd struck the final chord.

"Thanks." He laid the guitar on the bed. "But not as beautiful as you," he said, touching her breast.

And he drew her willingly into his arms and made love to her again with the unhurried tenderness she deserved.

Chris let Madelyn know that she could spend the night, but she insisted that if she didn't return to the dorm, her friends would worry. Besides, she had an early lab the next morning. Being on campus would make it easier to get there on time.

After Chris took her back to the campus on the bus, he walked home. It took a long time, but he felt as if he needed it to think things through. Making love to Madelyn had been wonderful, but now that they'd done it, he wasn't sure what direction he should take.

She definitely wasn't the kind of girl who went in for cheap one-nighters. Would she expect him to marry her or something?

Probably not. She hadn't said anything to make him feel she expected him to commit himself to a lifelong relationship. On the other hand, the way she'd looked at him while

they lay in bed after making love—almost worshipfully...
Well, that was enough to send any guy running in a panic.

An insidious fear clutched at his stomach. It wasn't that she might expect a future with him that he couldn't give. This was worse. She thought he was as good as she was... even better. She was putting him up on some damn pedestal. To her, he was a talented classical musician, a serious scholar and beloved son of a respectable citizen. Everything he'd told her about his past had built an image he couldn't hope to live up to!

Chris couldn't believe Madelyn would feel the same way about the real Chris McGuire. Now what was he going to do?

He stomped along the pavement in a daze, his stomach tying itself in bigger and bigger knots the farther he walked. Somehow he found his way to the front of his apartment building. The early October air was chilly and invigorating. He thought that maybe, if he sat outside long enough, he could come up with a solution.

He had no idea how much time passed before a voice interrupted his agonized thoughts.

"Do you realize it's after eleven o'clock and forty degrees out here, McGuire?"

His head snapped up, and his eyes met Becky's. "Eleven? Really?"

"Yeah, are you coming up?" she asked. "Or are you going to sit here and wait for the first snow?"

He couldn't even force a smile in response to her gentle teasing. "I have some things to think through," he said.

She sat down beside him, wrapping herself in her tidy gray all-weather coat and tucking her hands between her knees. It occurred to him that although Becky Delaney's reddish brown hair and vibrant green eyes contrasted sharply with Madelyn's light brown hair and eyes, the two girls had a lot in common. Both were shy and intelligent. Both came from

the Midwest, were conservative by nature and had delicately framed bodies. Becky wanted to lose her job in the personal ads department at the funky alternative newspaper *Chicago Now* and become a reporter, while Madelyn had spoken wistfully of becoming a novelist.

With so much in common, maybe Becky could give him an easy solution to his problem.

"It's Madelyn, the girl I've been seeing," he said, staring at his hands.

"From what Jessica and C.J. said, I thought things were working out really well for you two," she said softly.

He shifted his position on the hard stone stoop. "That's just it. We're...well, we're closer than ever. I'm in love with her, Beck. I'm head over freakin' heels in love with her."

"And what about her?"

"I think it's the same for her. She's the most honest person I've ever met. I don't think she knows how to fake an emotion. I can see it in her eyes when we... when we make love."

Becky nodded, smiling at him. "Congratulations. She sounds like just what you need, Chris."

He shook his head violently. "Maybe she's what I need, but I'm not what she needs."

"What's that supposed to mean?"

"I'm not even in the same class as Madelyn. I'm like..." He struggled to find the right words, raking his fingers through the long strands of black hair falling over his eyes. "She's this perfect girl, you know? I can tell she's never done anything wrong or stupid in her whole life. She loves classical music, hanging out in museums and at art shows, going to concerts—and I'm not talking about heavy-metal rock, either."

"And you're a talented musician who's going to have a degree in psychology," she pointed out.

"No. That's not me. That's part of what I'd like to be, but I'm light-years away. Meanwhile, I'm still a loser, and I haven't got anything that's really me to offer her."

"You're not a loser. You're just like the rest of us, struggling to make the future happen. You said you love her," Becky pointed out. "That's a lot."

Chris gritted his teeth. "It's not enough for a girl like Madelyn. She ought to be with someone who can take her to the symphony and know what the hell they're playing. Someone who isn't the son of the town drunk."

Becky laid a her hand on his arm. "You aren't giving yourself enough credit, Chris."

He groaned. "Everything might be okay... except, like I told you before, I went and told her all this stuff about studying classical guitar, being a full-time student and coming from this great family who's always there for me."

"So tell her the truth. You don't know how she'll react to the real you. Maybe she'll like you even better."

He let out a sharp laugh, his misery building. "Fat chance! Besides, telling her the truth now will only be admitting to her that I lied to her from the start. I have a feeling that honesty's pretty high on her list of desirable character traits for boyfriends."

"And what happens when she finally finds out the truth on her own and realizes you've intentionally deceived her?" Becky asked.

A jolt of terror ripped through Chris. He'd lose Madelyn—that's what would happen. She'd walk out of his life, taking with her the purest sunshine he'd ever known.

"I guess I'll have to deal with that when the time comes," he murmured disconsolately.

But as the days passed, Chris began to feel less anxious about Madelyn's discovering the real Christopher McGuire. They met at her dorm or his place almost every day,

almost always during the days, since he had to work most nights. He began to feel as if he could successfully balance his two lives.

There was his life when he was alone—practicing riffs and runs on his Fender, blasting the neighbors and playing out his guts. Later, he'd take off to tend bar at Razzles and gossip with the trendy crowd.

And then there was the subdued, latest model Chris who bought a new pair of jeans so he'd have two pairs that weren't torn, who shaved every day, who escorted his lady to listen to a string quartet at Symphony Hall and to stroll through dozens of galleries in River North and oooh over a collection of English watercolors, who memorized romantic poetry to recite to her and transposed a Schumann sonata written for harpsichord so he could play it for her on the acoustic guitar.

They made love every time they were together. Although his stomach balled up in a fierce knot every time he embellished one of his fibs, he began to believe he could ignore his aching gut if it meant keeping his Madelyn.

Madelyn lay in his arms, breathing softly. Chris pulled the sheet up over them and kissed her gently on the cheek. Her eyes closed and she smiled.

"That was wonderful," she murmured.

He could almost see the high of her ecstacy waning, giving way to a limp, sexually sated woman.

"You always say that after we make love," he teased. "A person who wants to become a writer ought to be able to come up with something more original."

"There are no words to describe how you make me feel when we make love," she whispered throatily, her eyes as bright as stars.

GETTING REAL: CHRISTOPHER   113

Her hand came up behind his head, coaxing him down toward her until their lips touched. She tasted warm, salty and pungent with sex.

"You're like potato chips," he said, laughing. "I can't stop."

Madelyn giggled, gazing up at him with deep pleasure in her eyes. "I'm afraid we have to. I have two exams to study for tonight."

"I have homework, too," he admitted. "I'll make some coffee for us." Despite his good intentions, though, he didn't move from her side. She and the bed smelled too good, felt too good.

He moved over her, immediately aroused by the sensation of her breasts against his chest and her naked body stretched out beneath him. Her words might have been sensible, but he knew from the dark sparks in her eyes that her need for him had been reawakened, too. She looped her soft arms around his neck and pulled him to her, opening her mouth sweetly to his.

He lifted his hips, and she gazed up at him in sweet anticipation of his entering her when a loud knock rattled the front door.

Chris dropped his forehead in exasperation against Madelyn's. "C.J., I'm going to kill you!" he bellowed.

Madelyn giggled good-naturedly. "I'm going to have to meet this girl and tell her to lay off my boyfriend."

The knock came again, louder.

"C.J., get lost!" Chris shouted, louder. The girl was really becoming a monster pest. Maybe her crush on him was getting out of hand. Was she intentionally trying to interrupt their intimate moments?

This time the pounding sounded strong enough to break down the door.

"She must be on a major sugar high," Chris grumbled, ready to strangle his neighbor as soon as he reached the door.

"It's all right, Chris," Madelyn said. "Just let her in. I'll get dressed and come out. I'd like to meet her."

"If she's still alive," Chris muttered, hopping on one foot toward the front door as he attempted to stuff one leg into his jeans.

He zipped the fly and unlocked the door. "This is ridiculous!" he shouted before the door swung into him with such force, it nearly knocked him flat.

Into the room staggered a tall man with a red face and wide, slumped shoulders. He was dressed in a rumpled cloth jacket and baggy chinos.

"Dad!" Chris choked out.

"Damn!" Jake McGuire swore, glaring around the room through squinted eyes. "Where's the can? I gotta take a leak bad!"

Chris stepped in front of him, blocking his path. His father had been to his apartment a couple of times, and it was only a matter of seconds before he'd remember the floor plan.

"You have to leave," Chris rasped out. He could hear water running and knew that Madelyn was in the bathroom. "I have company."

"Company?" Jake beamed at his son. "Good, we'll have a p-p-party," he slurred.

Chris turned his face away from the sickening stench of booze on his father's breath. He braced his hands on the man's shoulders.

"Dad, you have to leave now. I'll call you at home. How did you get here?" The rattletrap of a car he'd been driving had been repossessed months ago.

"Took the bus!" his dad proclaimed with pride.

"Good, you can take it home again." Chris fished in his pocket for a five. "Here, take this. Call me when you get home so I'll know you're okay."

By then he'd have taken Madelyn back to the dorm and be at the apartment to receive his call. He shoved Jake toward the front door while his father complained and dragged his feet, making the process difficult but not impossible.

Then something caught Jake's eye. He put on the brakes and, with drunken agility, slipped past Chris and back into the living room. "Well, who do we have here?" he asked.

Chris spun around. To his horror, Madelyn stood there, dressed in her neatly pressed jeans and favorite oxford shirt. She observed the scene with a puzzled expression.

"You have to leave," Chris repeated urgently. "You'll miss your bus!" He lunged for his father's arm, but the man jerked away from him and staggered toward Madelyn with his hand extended.

"How d-d-do you do?" he slurred formally. "I'm Jake... Jake McGuire. Don't believe we've had the plea... sure." The last word was interrupted by a resounding burp.

Madelyn stared at him, then at Chris, before turning back to Jake and shaking hands. "I'm Madelyn Phillips, Chris's friend."

"Some friend!" Jake shouted, eyeing her appreciatively. "You my Chrissy's current squeeze?" He wiggled his thick eyebrows suggestively.

Madelyn blushed and looked at Chris.

"He's my uncle," Chris blurted out. "Don't mind him. He's always drunk." He grabbed Jake firmly by the back of his jacket and steered him unceremoniously toward the door.

With an unexpected burst of strength, Jake shook him off and spun on him. "Yer uncle, my ass! You no-good lyin'

kid!" He jabbed a finger into Chris's bare chest. "I'm your old man, and don't you never forget it, hear?"

The bottom fell out of Chris's stomach. He didn't dare look at Madelyn to see the expression on her face. He felt the world come tumbling down around him, and there was nothing he could do to put it right again.

"Why'd you come here?" Chris asked wearily.

His father pouted, his dark eyes the color of his son's but they were unhealthily glazed and looked tiny in his bloated face. "I came to ask you a favor. To ask my *only son* a favor—is that so bad?"

"What?" Chris bit off.

"I'm sorta short this month and I was wondering if—"

"I just gave you four hundred to pay the rent!" Chris burst out. "What happened to that?"

His father straightened his shoulders and observed him indignantly. "I paid the rent. But a man's gotta eat, don't he?"

"Your job!" Chris ground out between clenched teeth. "That's why you have a freakin' job, man! To pay for groceries and stuff."

Jake sighed deeply and studied the toes of his scuffed work boots. "I been sorta laid off."

Chris felt as if he'd explode. He was no longer aware of Madelyn in the room. All he could see was the disgusting, drunken slob of a man he couldn't shove out of his life... because they were blood. Jake was his father, and Chris knew with a sinking heart that he'd never be free of his old man or his past.

"You've been laid off or fired?" Chris demanded.

His father shrugged. "Don't matter." A gleam of indignation momentarily brightened his eyes. "Crummy management types. A man misses a few days of work cause he's sick, and they dump him."

"Did you call in? Did you even *tell* them you were sick, or did you just not show up for a week like at the other places?" Chris demanded, furiously.

"I dunno." Jake scowled, looking puzzled. "I thought I called, but—"

Chris didn't wait for him to finish. He was already on his way into the kitchen, yanking open cupboard doors and pulling out cans of baked beans, soup and Spam. "The bathroom's in there—go ahead and use it," he shouted, shoving cans into a brown paper bag.

Two minutes later, Chris recrossed the living room, avoiding Madelyn's eyes, and met Jake as he came back through the room. He thrust the bag into his father's arms.

"I don't have any money, Dad. Take the food. At least this way you won't blow the cash on booze, and you'll get some decent food into you for a couple of days." He was so furious, he couldn't think straight. It was all he could figure out to do at the moment.

Jake cast him a disappointed look but moved obediently toward the door, yawning as he plodded across the carpet. The alcohol was evidently running its usual course. In less than an hour he'd be out cold.

"Tell your street to the bus driver when you get on," Chris said, his voice softer. "He'll wake you up at your stop."

"Don't worry 'bout me," Jake grumbled, jerking around to stomp out the door. "I can take care of myself. Don't need any bratty kid tellin' me what to do."

Chris watched him stumble down the hall, still muttering to himself. He pushed the elevator button and got on when the doors opened.

Minutes after his father had disappeared from the corridor, Chris stood looking out into the empty hall, feeling the pain in his gut swell until it filled his whole body.

He had to turn around and face Madelyn. He had to look her in the eye and answer the questions she'd demand answers for. He dreaded the moment more than death itself.

Nine

"Chris?" Madelyn's voice came to him through his agony.

He turned around slowly.

She had her coat on, her knapsack slung over one thin shoulder. "I'm going now."

"Please don't," he begged frantically. "I didn't want you to know about—"

"About your father? You were ashamed of your father?" she demanded, staring at him accusingly.

"Yeah, I mean... who wouldn't be?"

She shook her head. "You made up a family that didn't exist. What sort of scam are you working, Chris? Was it all to get me into bed?"

"It's not like that at all!" he cried, rushing toward her, needing to take her in his arms and keep her from leaving.

She dodged to one side and streaked toward the door.

"Wait!" he cried. "I'm sorry. I just didn't want you to know about him until the time was right. Until we got to know each other better."

"Oh, really!" she spat. "And how am I supposed to get to know you when you create a pretend Chris? How many other ways have you tricked me?"

"I haven't... wouldn't!" he protested desperately.

She looked at him, her eyes as sharp as chipped obsidian. "Do you think I'm blind? Do you think I'm stupid?"

"No!" he gasped.

She shook her head violently and stamped her foot at him. "I just opened your closet door, looking for a clean towel," she shouted. "Instead I found an electric guitar, amplifiers and heavy-rock sheet music. And what about the way you always change the subject when I ask about Ramone's? Do you even work at the place? Does it even exist? None of *my* friends have ever heard of it!"

"Madelyn, please!" he wailed.

She grasped the knob and yanked open the door with a furious jerk from her whole body.

"I'll call you tomorrow," he promised. "Everything will be fine. It's just a little misunderstanding—"

"Don't bother," she tossed over her shoulder as she swung through the door and slammed it in her wake.

That night, Chris couldn't sleep. He threw himself out of bed the next morning at 5:00 a.m., feeling as if he'd been dragged for miles behind a speeding motorcycle. The bruises to his soul were deep and real; he hurt with a physical intensity he hadn't known since his mother died.

For two hours he rattled around in the apartment, picking up his notes for the English project, then throwing them down in disgust without reading them. He couldn't bear to look at Shelley's words of love; they reminded him of Madelyn.

He took out the Fender. Without plugging it in, so he wouldn't wake his neighbors, he strummed a few poignant minor chords, before laying it aside.

He had no interest in playing. All that mattered was Madelyn, and she'd left him.

Pulling on his black leather jacket, he hit the streets and started walking. The Loop was jammed with people headed for work. He started walking, without thinking about the direction. His body yearned for action; he stretched out his legs and ate pavement.

GETTING REAL: CHRISTOPHER

The air smelled of car exhaust and fresh coffee from the nearby restaurants. A nippy October morning breeze slipped off Lake Michigan and under his collar, making him shiver. His hands felt sweaty, but they also shook. He thrust them into his pockets, lowered his head and marched on wearing a brooding scowl. Pedestrians cast him wary looks and stepped out of his way.

He didn't pay much attention to where he was headed. Sometime later he found himself on the U. of C. campus, standing in front of Madelyn's dorm. Blinking at the grim Gothic structure that mirrored his mood, he drew his tongue across parched lips and forced himself to walk through the door.

Chris took the stairs, needing time to think. *If I tell her everything... about my past, about the band, tending bar, and only being a part-time student, maybe...*

"Jerk," he muttered to himself. That would just be digging his grave deeper. Every lie he admitted to would simply prove Madelyn's point—he'd created a make-believe character to impress her. Being straight with her now would accomplish nothing.

He knocked on her door, his mind still racing, still grasping at possibilities, when her clear, cool voice called out, "Come in."

Silently he stepped through the door. Sandy wasn't there, and Madelyn was stretched out on her bed in an oversize sweatshirt and black leggings. Her English text, notebook and assorted library books fanned out around her on the bedspread.

"What do you want?" she asked without looking up from her work.

"I...I came to apologize," he choked out.

"Not necessary," she murmured, tracing over a word on her notepad.

A feather-light quiver of hope teased Chris's stomach. "You mean, you're not mad anymore? It's okay with you and me?"

She looked up at him, her eyes cold and unrelenting. "Chris, I don't want to see you anymore."

He felt as if she'd kicked him in the groin. "What?" he gasped. "Because of last night? Because of my dad?"

She let out a long sigh. "You still don't understand, do you?" she asked grimly.

"Tell me!" he demanded desperately. "What's the big deal? You said yourself that your parents weren't that great. Always fighting, making your life miserable. They probably embarrassed you in front of friends sometimes."

"Of course they did. But this is different."

"How?" he shouted, crazy with fear that she was really shutting him out forever.

"If you don't understand, I can't explain it to you," Madelyn said quietly. She stared at him, dry-eyed, but her hand betrayed her by trembling as she set to work again with her pen. "Please leave, Chris. I have work to do."

He spun around and slammed out of her room, rocketing down the stairwell and out into the morning air. It had started to rain... hard. Chris marched relentlessly through the downpour, ignoring the frigid droplets that stung his face and dribbled down inside his collar.

He hated himself more than he could ever hate another person. Why hadn't he been born the kind of guy who deserved a Madelyn in his life? Why?

For two weeks, Chris saw Madelyn only in English class. Her rigid posture in lecture hall and the classroom telegraphed a clear message to him: *Stay away from me!*

He did. He sat on the other side of the room from her, feeling outcast and alone. Other girls stopped by to flirt with him. At first, he tried to do his part by chatting about

whatever came to mind. But he felt hollow inside. ... himself comparing them with Madelyn. This one was ... almost boyish compared to Madelyn's delicate body. This one was dull-witted, with none of Madelyn's sparkling wit and intelligence. That one was too phoney...wore too much makeup...smoked...had ugly knees...chewed gum loudly...

There was always an excuse.

When he glanced across the room to see if Madelyn had noticed the attention he was getting, she was taking notes from a book. When their glances happened to meet, her cool brown eyes revealed no emotion and slipped away.

Three weeks after the fiasco at his apartment, Jimmy telephoned.

"Listen, man, I did everything you wanted. It's time," he said.

"What?" Chris asked, honestly at a loss.

Whatever had happened before Madelyn broke up with him seemed as if it were part of someone else's life. Chris had slipped back into his work routine at Razzles, did his assigned homework and slept a lot more than usual without ever feeling rested—but none of those things required any thought.

"The band...man. Don't pull that amnesia bit with me," Jimmy raved. "I hired a new bassist *and* got a keyboard man. The guy's, like, unbelievable. He can play *anything!* And I've been writing some new numbers for us."

Slowly Chris's mind began to churn, working its way back into familiar territory. "You wrote new songs?"

"Yeah, you gotta hear them. Two have super dance beats—driving, man. And the other...well, it's different from anything else we've ever done, but it's not totally finished. I have the lyrics and parts of the melody, but it needs a little more work." He let out a wry laugh. "Maybe I'm getting old, but it sounds like something my mom would like. One of those mushy ballads, you know?"

GETTING REAL: CHRISTOPHER

Chris laughed. Jimmy was twenty-three, hardly a senior citizen. "What about the gigs?" he asked.

"I've got two lined up for sure, and a third possibility. They're all private parties, but we're getting paid up front."

"How about getting your message across?" Chris asked.

Jimmy hesitated. "Well, I gave that some thought, see. It's like, I'm not totally sure what my message is. I mean, there's a lot of garbage going down in the world—pollution, disease, wars and stuff—and I want to see that go away. But I figure we can't tackle everything at one time and expect anyone to listen to us. That'd be a total downer."

"So?" Chris prodded gently.

"For now, let's just play some good music," Jimmy said. "We'll help people have a good time. When I figure out how we can make a real difference, I'll write a song that means something, instead of whining about everything in general."

Chris smiled to himself. Could it be Jimmy was growing up? "Sounds good to me," he murmured.

"Then you'll come back? You'll start practicing with us?"

"Sure. When's the first gig?"

"A week from Friday...and the second is the following Friday, with a possible on that Saturday."

"Cool," Chris said, "I'll rearrange my work schedule."

Chris missed Madelyn more than he could have explained to anyone or rationalized to himself. When he bumped into his neighbors in the hall he didn't put off their questions, but he didn't get into a lengthy explanation, either.

"We split up," he said abruptly.

Jessica looked at C.J., then at him. "She didn't like the real you?"

He shrugged. Let her think he'd tried to come clean and it hadn't worked out. That was less painful than admitting to her that she'd been right. Everything had blown up in his face.

Besides, he was getting his life back together. It felt good to play his kind of music again, to forget about always wearing something clean and hole-free. It felt good to not have to shave every day and to let his hair grow out so that it warmed the back of his neck as the days grew cooler. He told himself that he liked having the whole day to rattle around in, not having to schedule Razzles, band practices and schoolwork around the times when Madelyn was free. Life was simpler again. He hadn't vacuumed the apartment since the day she walked out in a huff, and he didn't give a damn. Let the dust pile up! No one was there to scrunch up her feminine nose in distaste.

"What about that third song?" Chris asked Jimmy after they'd been working for a couple of hours, polishing up their set for the party that Friday.

"Like I said, it's really not finished," Jimmy said.

"Let me see it. We need a change of pace after 'Flat Jammin' and 'Restless.'"

Jimmy handed him the sheet music with penciled-in notes and scrawled lyrics beneath them. Chris took the pages over to the beat-up sofa in Jimmy's basement and stretched out with his guitar across his stomach.

Jimmy was trying to coordinate a vocal passage on "Restless" with Steve on the drums and Paul and Kurt, their new bass and keyboard men. Chris was only vaguely aware of their false starts and broken passages as they worked and reworked the troublesome spot, sweating out the rhythm and intricate patterns of notes.

He read Jimmy's lyrics in a low whisper.

"You waken my nights;
   you sleep in my days.
You fill me with love;
   I hunger for more.
Never, oh, never has there
   been a time—
When life was so good to me,
   or I've cried so hard.
Love me forever...
   forever, my love."

Chris closed his eyes and shut out the returning wave of loneliness. *Madelyn. Why couldn't you love me for who I am?* his heart shouted.

Furious with himself for letting her steal back into his heart, he pushed himself up off the sofa.

"Hey, man—this is good! This will work." He grabbed the pencil out of Jimmy's hand and erased a couple of notes, then added some new chords in the bridge of the song, "Cried So Hard."

"Right here is where we want the riff on the lead guitar." He pointed to a bar of music. "Then Steve comes in here heavy with the drums."

Jimmy frowned. "You sure? This is a ballad. We don't want to slam our way through it."

"It won't come out like that. Stoking up the volume will add emotion to the song. You're talking about pain here, man. We have to *hear* the pain—so a riff and drums."

Kurt looked over Chris's shoulder. "He's right. It was too subtle. The changes will make it real. Let's give it a shot."

Jimmy nodded and patted Chris on the back. "Why don't you sing this one?" he asked.

"I don't sing for performances," Chris reminded him dryly.

"You haven't yet, but you got a pretty decent voice, and your baritone suits this song better than my blues rasp."

Chris smiled, shaking his head. "I'll pass. You're the vocalist in the group."

"Suit yourself." Jimmy looked around at the others. "Let's do it."

Madelyn walked out of the gymnasium and her second aerobics class of the day. She'd decided after her breakup with Chris that she needed more exercise, something to keep her mind off of him in the spare moments between classes, homework, meals and sleeping.

She'd started out taking one high-impact class, three days a week with Sandy. Then she'd added others on the off days. But she became so restless waiting until evening to go with her roommate, she'd decided to add a morning session whenever her classes allowed.

Now, after a couple of weeks of the grueling routine, she'd lost five pounds she didn't need to lose, but was beginning to feel as if she could at least cope emotionally with the rest of her life. She walked into her room to find Sandy and Cassie discussing a party.

"Hi," she said shortly, flinging her coat on the bed.

The two girls looked at her.

"My God! What are you trying to do to yourself?" Cassie demanded ogling her leotard-clad figure. "You're all bones! Have you been eating at all?"

"Of course I am," Madelyn said huffily, pulling on sweats before plopping into her desk chair and putting on her reading glasses. "You think I'm going to let some guy screw up my health?"

Sandy made a face at her. "I think you've been a neurotic wreck since you and Chris split up."

Madelyn shrugged. "And you handled your breakup so well. Besides, he left me no choice."

"I didn't say you were wrong to leave him," Sandy stated. "I just said you're not handling it too cool."

Madelyn pushed her books aside on her desk and picked up a mug of cold coffee. She took a sip of the bitter liquid laced with Sweet'n Low and powdered creamer.

"Okay," she blurted out angrily, "you tell me how you'd handle some guy who'd lied to you, some guy who'd made you trust him, believe in him and—"

"Fall in love with him?" Cassie added with a wise glint in her pretty eyes.

"I never said I was in love with him," Madelyn said bitterly.

"You never said you weren't."

Madelyn shrugged. "Anyway, it doesn't matter. He was too good to be true, I should have been smart enough to see that. We liked all the same things—art, opera, poetry, white pizza." She shook her head. "And all the time he was using me."

Sandy moved across the room and knelt down beside her. "What was he using you for, sex?"

Madelyn's chin shot up, and she looked away from her roommate. "What else? Isn't that what they all want?"

Cassie let out a long sigh and pursed her lips thoughtfully. "Then that's not why you were interested in him. You didn't particularly like the sex?"

"That's not the point!" Madelyn gasped.

"Maybe... maybe not. He didn't force you to have sex with him, right?"

"Right. But he built himself up to be something he—"

"So you thought he liked Brahms better than Megadeth? What's the big deal?" Sandy patted Madelyn's knee affectionately. Her blue eyes were solemn. "Are you afraid of meeting someone who isn't a male Madelyn?"

Madelyn let out a shriek of indignation and stood up abruptly, knocking Sandy on her tush.

"I realize that people are different!" Madelyn snapped. "If Chris ate worms for breakfast, sang rap music from morning till night and shaved his head, it wouldn't matter to me!"

Cassie lifted her brows. "It sure would matter to me!"

"Well, of course, it might make me think he was a little strange. But the rest of Chris, all the nice things he is, how gentle, considerate and smart in a natural way—all that wouldn't change. I'd still care for him."

Sandy scowled at her, obviously puzzled.

"Don't you see?" Madelyn begged. "He *lied* to me about almost everything that mattered to him in his life. His father, his music—which I suspect is a lot different from what he said he liked. He was trying to hide something from me!"

"Do you *know* what he was trying to hide?" Cassie asked.

"Not really. It's not like I hired a private eye to follow him or anything. But, now that I think back, there was always a strange sort of tension in everything he said and did, as if he had to be very careful what he told me. And there were all the nights we couldn't be together, because he claimed he had to work. I looked up Ramone's in the Yellow Pages and it's not listed. What kind of restaurant doesn't put its phone number in the book?"

"Maybe there was another girl," Sandy suggested gently.

Madelyn nodded numbly. "I've thought of that." She wished her friends would quit pumping her for information. She just wanted to be left alone to forget and heal. "I expect there must have been at least one other girl," she admitted. "They always throw themselves at him in English class. It's probably like that everywhere he goes. You met him," she said to Sandy, as if that summed up everything.

"He is awfully good-looking," her roommate admitted. "But that doesn't mean he was unfaithful to you. Maybe you're just too insecure to trust him?"

Madelyn shook her head. "That's just the problem. I did trust him, and I was a fool. But I won't set myself up for that kind of killer heartbreak again," she swore with a shake of her head.

Cassie sighed. "Well, some guys just aren't worth the agony. So... how about going out with a bunch of us tomorrow night?"

"I have a lot of work to do," Madelyn said quickly.

"Eighteen hours a day of work is enough. You need a break."

"But I—"

"You *are* going out with us," Sandy insisted. "It's just a frat party—no big deal. You'll meet a bunch of guys—most of whom are total jerks and will get wasted before the night's over. But sometimes there are a few who hang out in dark corners and blush when a girl looks at them. Just your type. Totally nonthreatening."

They sounded boring to Madelyn. "I don't know."

"I'm teasing." Sandy laughed. "We'll go together and have fun. You need to find someone to help you forget about Chris. Believe me, I've done it dozens of times, and it always works. Out with the old, in with the new!"

Madelyn sighed, staring at her roommate doubtfully. "All right, I'll go if it'll make you happy. But the first guy who pukes on me, I'm out of there."

Ten

Madelyn trailed after Sandy down the dark stairwell and into Pi Sigma Delta's basement. Cassie brought up the rear, as if to make sure Madelyn didn't chicken out at the last minute. A cloud of cigarette smoke rose up to meet her, along with the stench of beer.

"Karen! Hey, Wanda! Chris!" Sandy shouted excitedly from the bottom step. "Isn't this setup wild?"

At the last name, Madelyn jumped and automatically peered around the dimly lit room, envisioning *her* Chris. But Sandy had been shouting to one of the girls from their dorm, and the surge of bittersweet emotions through her nerves seeped away again, leaving her feeling disappointed and grateful at the same time. After all, she couldn't have faced Chris in a place like this, with all these people around.

Madelyn looked around the room. It was large with dark paneling, and it had an open, smooth-vinyl floor for dancing. There were plenty of folding chairs arranged around the walls. At the far end, a platform had been erected, and a couple of scraggly-looking musicians were setting up speakers and running electrical cords.

At the end nearest the stairs was a long metal table—the collapsible kind reminiscent of school cafeterias—covered with a paper tablecloth in a circus motif. There was a huge punch bowl, and paper cups in bright primary colors that reminded Madelyn of her first set of chunky Crayola crayons. Plates of cookies and brownies, and bowls of chips

ranged across the paper covering. Crepe paper streamers and balloons hung from the ceiling.

The effect was so zanily cheerful, Madelyn couldn't help laughing out loud. "I haven't been to a party like this since third grade!"

Sandy turned to her. "Great, isn't it?" She pointed to a keg of beer on a stool in the corner. "I don't think we had one of those, though."

"True."

"It's sort of retrochildhood," Cassie put in. "You're supposed to bring or wear something that you had when you were a kid."

"I didn't know." Madelyn sighed. She noticed that Wanda wore a baby's pacifier on a pink ribbon around her neck.

As she checked out other guests, she spotted a few who carried baby bottles that looked as if they were filled with something other than milk. One girl wore a frilly bonnet tied in a bow around her neck. There was a guy in oversize Osh-Kosh B'Gosh overalls, a couple of other guys with Nerf balls and bats, a girl in pigtails adorned with enormous polka-dot bows, and someone riding a tricycle.

"You didn't tell me it was going to be a theme party," Madelyn complained.

Sandy laughed. "You wouldn't have come if I had. Anyway, it'll be fun! Here—" She reached into her purse and pulled out two pairs of garish plastic sunglasses decorated with cartoon characters at the hinges.

Madelyn eyed them skeptically. "You've got to be kidding...."

Her roommate grinned at her.

Maybe Sandy was right. Maybe she needed to do something outrageous to help her put Chris out of her mind and heart. "Oh, all right. But I get Scooby Doo!" she cried, snatching the pink pair out of Sandy's hand.

"That's more like it. Now, let's get something to drink and eat before the good stuff's gone. But look out for the punch. You don't know what's in there!"

"You're on."

Madelyn put on her plastic glasses. The lenses were so dark and the light in the basement was so faint, all she could see were shadows of people moving back and forth across her line of vision. She thought the place looked much less weird this way and decided to keep them on.

Suddenly the band started playing. The music was loud, the beat pulsating, encouraging guests to move to the center of the floor and dance. Immediately, half a dozen couples set down beers and polished off brownies to answer the music's call.

Madelyn tipped her glasses down and peered over the frames but couldn't see between the dancers to get a good look at the musicians' faces. But it seemed that no attempt had been made to coordinate their costumes. Some wore jeans, one wore leather, two others were garbed in pleated, baggy trousers and bright-colored vests.

"Want to dance?" a voice asked.

Madelyn whipped around to face a young man wearing a wild, flower-patterned shirt. She opened her mouth to say no, then realized he was looking at Sandy...not her.

"Sure!" her roomie chirped. "Why not?" And she gave Madelyn a meaningful look as she swung past her and onto the dance floor.

"'Sure! Why not?'" parroted Madelyn, snatching up a huge chocolate-chip cookie. "I can say that. Simple!" Like she didn't care that the only boy she wanted to dance with was Chris. *Why did he have to be such a fake?* she thought, collapsing into an empty chair and chomping down on the cookie.

The band played two more numbers, and Madelyn ate two more cookies. They tasted like beach sand in her mouth.

She was starting on her third when she glimpsed a guy moving across the room in her direction. He wore neatly pressed trousers of a soft brown or gray—she couldn't tell which from behind the sunglasses—a conservative, light-colored shirt and a striped Ivy League-style tie. He looked just her type: quiet, tidy, intelligent. She thought she remembered having seen him in a couple of her classes.

Her stomach tightened as she watched him work his way across the crowded room, looking straight at her. There was no mistaking his intent. He was going to ask her to dance.

Madelyn set the uneaten portion of her cookie on the chair next to her. She removed her glasses and lowered them to her lap. Sandy was right. She had to get on with her life. She'd told Chris in no uncertain terms that she wanted out of their relationship.

So she was out.

Maybe she'd never had the kind of social life most girls had. So what if she'd dated only infrequently before Chris came along. She could at least dance with this guy, maybe strike up a pleasant conversation. Who knows, she thought, he might be really nice.

He stopped in front of her and gave her a friendly smile. "I like your glasses."

She tilted her head to one side and looked up at him, attempting to smile back. "Thank you." Her eyes drifted across him quickly. "You don't have any props."

"No," he said with an embarrassed laugh. "I don't go in much for this sort of thing. In fact," he continued, glancing with irritation at the band when they cranked up the volume on the next song. "I don't know why I'm here. I can't stand this kind of music."

"Really?" she said. "Actually, I liked one of their earlier numbers. I think it just takes some getting used to." She noticed that the lead singer had a husky voice that tended to

muffle the words, but he added an appealing texture to the music that a classic tenor could never achieve.

"I was wondering if you'd like to dance," he said politely.

"Oh..." Say yes! Say yes! the little Sandy voice inside of Madelyn prompted. He's just your type. Proper manners, spotless dresser. Your parents would adore him. "No," she said meekly. "No, thank you."

He looked deflated.

"Hey, it isn't you," she said quickly. "I..." She stuck out her hand to shake his, wanting to make him feel better. The music pumped up a couple of hundred decibels, and she had to shout to be heard over it. "My name is Madelyn. I'm glad to meet you. You're...?"

"Jerry. Jerry Filmore. Third year student."

"I'm sorry, Jerry. I just don't feel like dancing tonight. My girlfriend talked me into coming because I was feeling kind of down. She thought a party would help, or something...I don't know." She shook her head miserably.

"It's some guy, isn't it?" Jerry asked in a calm voice that somehow penetrated the noise.

"Yeah. I'm just having a hard time getting over him. How did you know?"

"I have three older sisters." He laughed knowingly. "I recognize the symptoms."

"Thanks for asking anyway," Madelyn said, smiling at him. "Maybe another time."

"Well," Jerry said, "don't let him keep you out of circulation for too long. There are a lot of guys who'd kill to take out a special girl like you. And we're not all creeps like your old boyfriend."

She opened her mouth, then stopped herself before she could defend Chris. After all, Jerry was right. Chris had taken advantage of her in the worst possible way—he'd stolen her heart.

She watched Jerry walk away, linger near the refreshment table, then glance once more across the dark room. A few minutes later, he climbed the basement stairs, and she knew he wouldn't be back.

"He's got the right idea," she mumbled to herself.

She scanned the room, looking for Sandy, aching to leave too. The willowy blonde was dancing with a tall guy up near the bandstand. Madelyn stood and motioned to her, wanting to let her know she was leaving. But there were so many people dancing she could only catch an occasional glimpse of Sandy, and then it was impossible to capture her attention through the crowd and noise.

Madelyn hitched her purse over one shoulder, put the glasses back on and pushed her way between gyrating couples toward the rear wall of the room. The closer she got, the louder the music grew. She felt the vibrations of the drumbeat and bass guitar through the soles of her shoes. They traveled up through her legs, reaching inside her. It was a sexy feeling; she tried to shut it out but couldn't. Her breath puffed shallowly into her lungs, and she felt tears welling up in her eyes.

I have to get out of here! she thought hopelessly. *This just isn't working!*

At last she reached Sandy and grabbed her by the arm. The girl whirled around, her party smile collapsing into a puzzled frown when she saw Madelyn's face.

"What's wrong?" she gasped.

Unable to choke out anything resembling words, Madelyn shook her head and pointed toward the stairs.

"Hey, don't bail out yet!" Sandy shouted. "We just got here."

"You s-s-stay!" Madelyn stuttered, tears trickling from beneath her lashes. "I c-c-can't."

Sandy's partner rolled his eyes and walked away.

GETTING REAL: CHRISTOPHER

"Oh, I'm sorry!" Madelyn wailed. "Now you've lost your dance partner because of me."

"Forget him," Sandy said. "You *have* to stay. You'll never get over Chris if you don't see other guys. I won't let you keep moping around and starving yourself."

"I'll be okay, but I just don't want to be *here*. This isn't my kind of place," Madelyn pleaded. To make her point, she gestured toward the band. "Does this sound anything like my kind of music?" she demanded.

Following the wave of her own hand, she looked straight up at the lead guitarist... a young man with shaggy, black hair... piercing, dark eyes... an ebony leather vest and pleated pants to match.

With a strangled gasp, she whipped off her Scooby Doo glasses. Chris's head snapped up, and he stared at her as if he'd only just now recognized her, too.

"Oh, God, it's *him*," Sandy groaned.

Madelyn tossed the dark glasses at Sandy and shoved her way desperately between dancers, trying to reach the stairs and climb out of the room. Suddenly she felt as if she were trapped beneath fifty feet of water, unable to breathe, incapable of moving faster than dream pace—and her only chance of survival lay in scrambling to the surface.

She thought she heard Chris call out her name, but she kept on going.

It took Chris several seconds to recognize the slender, brown-haired girl hiding behind a goofy pair of kids' shades. In fact, he hadn't been focusing on much of anything during the band's first set. Most of the songs were from their old material and had become routine to him.

His fingers moved across the taut wires of his electric guitar of their own accord. His dark scowl only seemed to excite the girls who flocked around the platform.

But there was something going on just beyond his groupies that eventually caught his attention. He looked past the first few rows of dancers to two girls standing in the middle of the floor. One seemed oddly familiar from the back. Her hair was a pale, luminous blond, cut close to her head. Her super figure was shown off to its best advantage by her short skirt and fitted jersey.

He couldn't see the face of the other girl, because she was blocked by the blonde. But he could make out the sleeve of a soft pink sweater and one leg clad in tan corduroy. Then she stepped around the other girl, pulled off a pair of ridiculous sunglasses and stared straight at him.

Chris's heart rocketed into his throat. Somehow he'd imagined he'd never see Madelyn anywhere again but in English class...and he'd figured out ways of handling that. But running unexpectedly into her at a party shook him to the bottom of his soul.

She looked as if she'd spent the past few weeks shut in her room. She was pale and shaking, the lines of her pretty face pinched with pain. Her eyes glistened with tears.

He couldn't bear seeing her like that.

"Madelyn, wait!" he cried, letting his fingers drop away from the guitar.

The rest of the band continued playing.

Jimmy shot him a panicky look. "Hey, man, don't screw up! People are shoppin' new bands all the time! You want the gigs, don't you?"

Without answering him, Chris lifted his guitar strap up and over his head and hurriedly propped the instrument against a speaker. Jumping down from the platform, he jostled people aside to force his way through the crowd. He reached Madelyn just as she'd placed her foot on the bottom stair.

"Don't go!" he shouted again, this time inches from her ear.

GETTING REAL: CHRISTOPHER

She whipped around, a shocked look on her face as if she couldn't comprehend how he'd gotten from the other end of the room so fast.

"Please stay. I want to talk to you." Not taking any chances, he seized her arm and pulled her back into the room, then toward a corner. "I want to tell you some things about myself so you'll understand—"

"You've talked more than enough," she sobbed, angrily pushing his hands away. "I listened to you before! I trusted you!"

"Please," he begged, "give me one more chance. I promise I'll—"

"Get out of my life!" she screamed, wrenching her arm free.

For a second, Chris watched helplessly as she ran from him. He knew she wouldn't listen to him, not now, not as upset as she was. He wished with all his heart that he had some means of reaching her. Some way to get her attention that was untainted by the lies he'd told her before.

Chris drew a sharp breath and stared at Jimmy, who had picked up the Fender and was doing his best to keep up the dance beat with his limited playing experience. He had an idea. Just one idea that might blow up in his face... but he had to try.

Chris bolted back toward the front of the room and leapt onto the platform. He glanced the length of the room as he seized the guitar from Jimmy and ducked through the loop of the strap. Madelyn had finally reached the bottom of the stairs, but two couples were now using the bottom steps as seats and she was having trouble getting them to move for her.

"Fade into 'Cried So Hard!'" Chris shouted in Jimmy's ear.

"But we—"

"Do it, man! *I'll sing*—just do it for me, please...."

Jimmy shrugged. "You got it." He flashed five fingers twice for the other band members, indicating song number ten, which they'd originally planned to save for the next set.

Steve geared down smoothly into a ballad drumbeat, and the others followed his lead.

Chris shot a frightened glance across the room. Madelyn had at last succeeded in climbing over the stair sitters.

The gentle instrumental intro finished, and Chris forced out the first few words of the song, his voice tight with emotion.

"You waken my nights;
   You sleep in my days.
You fill me with love;
   I hunger for more... Madelyn."

To his horror, the waifish girl on the stairs kept on climbing, climbing. In a moment, she'd be gone, and there'd be no getting her back!

He sang out from the very depth of his soul.

"Never, oh, never has there
   been a time—
When life was so good to me,
   or I've cried so hard.
Love me forever...
   forever, my love... Madelyn."

Chris could no longer hold a note. His voice cracked as he shouted into the microphone, "I love you, Madelyn!"

Holding his breath, he watched as she hesitated, her back to him on the stairs, clutching the banister, still leaning forward and only three steps away from the top. Then she turned slowly and faced him across the heads of the watch-

ing guests. She sat down where she was and buried her face in her hands.

"Man, you're gonna get us fired," Jimmy muttered under his breath. "These frats want hot music, not a freakin' soap opera!"

"I owe you one," Chris gasped, knowing only that he'd bought himself a few precious minutes with Madelyn.

He handed Jimmy his guitar and raced across the floor then up the stairs in twos. Grabbing Madelyn by the shoulders, he lifted her gently to her feet.

"Let's go outside and walk," he said. "We need to talk about us."

She nodded limply.

From behind them, Chris could hear the band start up again. Jimmy was playing a simplified version of the lead guitar's part, and Kurt was filling in the melody on the keyboard.

Chris and Madelyn walked in silence down the street, past a couple of blocks of warehouses and toward the more scenic lakefront.

Chris's mind raced with each step. He remembered what Jessica and Becky had told him about leveling with Madelyn. He hadn't done it before because he'd been sure that she'd have nothing to do with him, and that he'd somehow find a way to charm her back into his arms.

Now he figured he had nothing to lose. Trying to be what he'd imagined she'd want in a guy hadn't worked.

At first Chris didn't dare look at her as they moved along the dark sidewalk, arms at their sides, not touching. But when he at last got up his courage to glance sideways at Madelyn, her face was tense and a sickly white, her brown eyes were bright with tears. He ached to wrap his arms around her and tell her that everything would be all right. But he had no way of knowing if he had the power to make anything right anymore.

After all, he hadn't succeeded in doing much with his life except enrolling as a part-time student and landing a job tending bar. Who was he to reassure her?

As they rounded the corner of the Acme warehouse, a sharp wind whipped off of Lake Michigan, hitting Chris in the face.

"So," Madelyn whispered into the sudden icy slap of air, "what do you have to tell me?"

"I want to tell you all about the real Chris McGuire," he forced out.

"So tell."

He stopped walking and turned her to face him, backing her into a doorway to escape the wicked gusts. Her shoulders were shaking, and he sensed that the trembling didn't stop there. Her delicate frame felt like a fragile flower weathering gale winds. At any minute she might bend and break.

"I need you to trust me one more time—" He broke off to press a hand over her mouth when he sensed she was going to interrupt him. "But it can't be tonight."

She glared at him. "If you have something more to say to me, say it now and get it over with. You have fifteen minutes. Then I'm going back to my room and I don't want to talk to you again, ever."

He shook his head. "No. You wouldn't understand if I just stood here and told you." He paused, allowing himself the treat of studying her for another minute, aware that each second they stood together might be their last. "Seeing is believing—that's what they say, right?"

"I guess," she said, a note of suspicion creeping into her voice.

"Good. I want you to see the real Chris McGuire. I want to give you a day in my life—all the good and bad, with the boring stuff in between."

Madelyn frowned. "I don't understand."

"Tomorrow's Saturday. I have a full day scheduled. The only thing that's not happening are classes...."

"But you told me you had Saturday labs—that was why we couldn't be together all Saturday!" she burst out.

"I know... I'm admitting that was a fabrication."

"A lie!" she spat out, her eyes glowing with indignation.

He groaned. "Okay... a lie. But I need you to see why I made up stories about myself. Please, spend Saturday with me. See who I really am. If you hate me at the end of the day, just tell me goodbye, and I'll get out of your life. Promise."

"And if I don't hate you? What if I like what I see... but you're still covering up, making up more lies for my benefit?"

"If you think that's what I've done, there's nothing I can do to convince you otherwise. I'll just have to trust your judgment."

The lump in Chris's throat felt as if it had swollen to the size of a grapefruit. He thought he heard Steve's drum, knocking out a queer rhythm in the distance; then he realized it was his own heart pounding thunderously in his chest. Chris ran his tongue between his dry lips.

"Well? What do you say? It's one day, that's all. If I disappoint you, you still have the rest of your life to look for a guy who meets your standards." He took a chance and reached out to take her hands in his. She didn't pull away. "What do you say?"

Madelyn drew a deep breath. "I'll know if you're lying this time, Chris," she warned.

"I know you'll know."

"I won't give in to charm this time," she warned sternly.

"I know you won't."

"I'm not a pushover or some little groupie who'll fall starry-eyed at your feet just because you happen to play loud, obnoxious rock music."

"Obnoxious?" he asked, frowning.

"Well, loud at least. It was awfully loud."

"I grant you that much," he said, allowing her a weak smile.

Madelyn dropped her eyes away from his, but her lips turned up, showing that she was warming to him just a little.

"I'll pick you up at eight o'clock tomorrow morning," he said, giving her fingertips an encouraging squeeze.

She withdrew her hands from his, as if she were afraid of allowing him the smallest satisfaction without proving himself. "Why so early?"

"We're taking my dad to breakfast...if we can roust him out of his drunken torpor."

She raised an eyebrow. "Sounds like a charming beginning to the day."

"You said you didn't want charming, you wanted reality," he reminded her. "Chickening out so soon?"

She straightened up and lifted her chin to glare at him, eye-to-eye. "Not a chance, Mr. McGuire. Dish up the works!"

"Good," he said, "that's exactly what I intend to do."

Eleven

Madelyn tossed and turned all night long. She picked up the telephone a half dozen times to call Chris and tell him to forget about picking her up.

She felt as if she were being drawn into a trap. Somehow Chris was going to convince her that he was the perfect guy for her. He'd probably take her to the Art Institute of Chicago, go on at length about a collection of Andrew Wyeth's watercolors—parroting facts he'd pulled out of an encyclopedia the night before. He'd tell her his playing was just a temporary thing, until a seat in the Chicago Symphony opened up. He'd charm her into believing he was a dedicated student, and take her to some posh bistro where he'd arrange for a friend to say he was a valuable employee.

It would all be such a sad waste of her time. She didn't think she could stand the emotional agony of going through such an involved ruse.

But every time Madelyn grabbed the receiver, she envisioned Chris's face. The finely chiseled, masculine features and the glint of determination in his dark eyes. The tousled, black hair that, endearingly, never seemed quite in place, even when he'd obviously taken great pains to comb it. The sound of his fingers singing across guitar strings. Oh, he'd poured magic into Bach...and her heart.

By morning she'd decided that, in all fairness, she owed herself one last day with Chris. Sadly, she'd probably never again run into anyone as interesting and exciting as he was. In a month or so, with Sandy and Cassie's prodding, she'd

start dating someone like Jerry, get engaged, then married, have three or four kids and never use her degree. Her life would be stable, safe, and she'd be comfortable enough in her little house somewhere in the suburbs.

But she'd never again know the thrill of making love with a man like Christopher McGuire.

She swallowed the flow of salty tears down the back of her throat and sniffled once as she tossed back her blankets and stood up on the fuzzy throw rug that lay between her and Sandy's beds.

Her roommate rolled over on her bed and squinted at her. "What are you doing up? Isn't it Saturday?"

"Yes," Madelyn said.

"What time is it, anyway?"

"Six."

"In the morning?"

With an fond smile, Madelyn pulled the covers up over Sandy's head. "Dream on, Sleeping Beauty. You don't have to get up. Besides, I'll probably be back here before noon. Then I can go back to bed, too, since there won't be anything else worth doing."

Sandy yanked down the sheets, sat up and stared at her. "You worry me when you talk like that. What's going on? I thought you and Chris got back together last night."

Madelyn shook her head. She hadn't had a chance to talk to Sandy after she and Chris went for their walk. She'd returned to the dorm and went to bed, then pretended to be asleep when Sandy got in hours later. Her mind and heart were torn in so many different directions, she couldn't have put her feelings into words.

"You know," Sandy muttered groggily, "I was shocked to see him there—boots, leather, a rock guitar... I thought Chris was totally into classical stuff and art."

"Like I told you, there seems to be another side to Mr. McGuire that I wasn't aware of," Madelyn said, arching a

brow at her. "And I'm supposed to get the whole show today."

Sandy fell back onto her pillow. "You're not coming home wearing leather and chains, are you?"

Madelyn wrinkled her nose at her. "I seriously doubt it."

Chris parked Jimmy's pickup on the street closest to Madelyn's dorm and jogged the rest of the way. She was waiting in the lobby, dressed in jeans, a white blouse with embroidered collar, her corduroy jacket and tan leather purse draped over one arm. She looked scrubbed clean but a little bleary-eyed, so he suspected she'd gotten no more sleep than the few hours he'd crammed in between anxiety attacks.

Chris ached to rush up to Madelyn, sweep her into his arms and kiss her the way they'd kissed at his apartment when they'd made love. But he knew she wouldn't welcome his embrace. He first had to win back her trust. Even then, there was no guarantee she'd like him the same way she had before—when he was a classical musician and promising full-time student. But it was a risk he had to take.

"Do buses run out to where your dad lives?" she asked, as they walked out through the glass doors into a sunny fall morning.

"We're driving," he explained. "Last night, after we took the equipment back to my friend's place, I borrowed his truck. There aren't any decent restaurants within walking distance of my dad's house."

"Oh," she said. Her tone made him wonder if she'd hoped he'd change his morning plans. "Is it far to his house?"

"Eldersdale's just a twenty-minute drive."

She nodded and accepted his offered hand to help her up into the truck's cab.

They drove for ten minutes without speaking. Chris could hold in his thoughts no longer.

"I promised this would be a day of truth, and I meant it. I called my dad last night from the frat house after you left, to tell him we'd be over this morning. I was sort of hoping he'd run out of cash and be sober, but he had a couple of buddies in the house and it sounded like they were sucking up the booze pretty fast."

Madelyn looked at him worriedly. "Maybe this isn't such a good idea. I mean, if he's asleep—"

"You mean, passed out?"

"Whatever...maybe we shouldn't intrude."

Chris shook his head. "He needs someone to intrude, to keep showing him there are ways to straighten out his life. Besides, you wanted the truth about me. I can't pretend I don't have a dad, and that he doesn't have problems."

She took a deep breath and nodded. "You're right."

Chris steered for the exit off the Tristate Tollway for Eldersdale. After driving along a short commercial strip lined with fast-food joints, dingy grocery stores and used-car dealers, he followed the familiar roads through the lower-class residential section to O'Connor Street. His dad's house was the fourth on the left. They pulled up beside the peeling, gray clapboard house.

"Looks like he's home," Chris commented tightly, seeing the screen door ajar and a light showing through the living room blinds.

He got out of the truck and came around to help Madelyn down from the high seat. Placing his hands around her tiny waist, he felt the tension in her muscles and in the way she gripped his shoulders as he eased her to the ground. She glanced nervously at the house, as if expecting a raving lunatic to burst through the front door at any moment and assault them. He couldn't blame her for being nervous after her first meeting with his dad.

"I'll go in first," Chris said when they reached the cement stoop outside the kitchen door. "Wait here a minute."

She nodded, her brown eyes wide.

Chris let himself in through the unlocked door and crossed the kitchen, which was littered with beer cans and dirty glasses. The sink brimmed over with filthy dishes—more than a week's worth, he estimated. The trash can overflowed with TV dinner cartons, more beer cans and cigarette butts. The place made his own housekeeping skills look pristine. It stunk to high heavens.

He rounded the corner into the living room and found his father in his favorite position—stretched out on his back on the grease-stained couch, an empty bottle of Scotch cuddled up in the crook of his arm. The classic drunk in his element.

With a sigh, Chris lifted the bottle out of the circle of his father's arm, then scooped up the half dozen beer cans littering the living room floor and returned to the kitchen.

"All clear!" he called out.

Madelyn peeked through the door and let her eyes roam the kitchen before stepping inside.

"If you'd rather wait in the truck—" Chris began, wondering if she was going to cut out on him this early in the day.

"No," she said quickly. "I'm fine. Where's your father?"

"Comatose on the couch."

"Oh. Well, what are we going to do since he's not ready for breakfast?"

"He'll be ready in fifteen minutes," Chris said grimly. He lifted a pile of old newspapers off of one of the two kitchenette chairs and tossed them into a garbage bag. "Have a seat," he said gesturing with a sweeping wave of his hand, as if he were offering her the best table at Maxim's.

Madelyn sat, her expression thoughtful as she studied the room around her.

Chris strode out of the kitchen, feeling his stomach knot inside of him. Bringing her here might have been a colossal mistake. So what if her parents bickered throughout her childhood. He doubted she'd been raised in a house that reeked of booze and decaying food and looked like a pigsty.

Chris seized his old man by the upper arms and hauled him into a sitting position.

"Come on, Dad!" he shouted in his ear. "Rise and shine!"

His father groaned, scrunching his eyes more tightly closed and smacking his mouth as if to get rid of the taste of the evening's beverages.

"We're taking you out for a nice hot breakfast," Chris informed him, dragging him to his feet. He sensed that the older man's knees were about to buckle, and so slung an arm under his shoulders to support him, and walked him toward the bathroom.

"Where we goin'?" Jake McGuire asked groggily.

"To the Pancake House, for breakfast."

"Not hungry," his father said firmly.

"You will be by the time we get you washed up and dressed. You have to be presentable. We have a lady guest."

His father opened his eyes for the first time and scowled at him. "There's a woman in my house?"

"In the kitchen. Let's not keep her waiting. You met her once at my apartment."

"I haven't been to your apartment in months!" Jake stated irritably.

"You don't remember, maybe, but you were there."

Chris set his father on the toilet cover and started the shower. When he'd adjusted the temperature, he helped his dad undress and pushed him under the steamy spray.

"Wash *everywhere*, with soap!" he shouted above the sound of the pelting water. "And shampoo your hair while you're at it."

"You sound like I'm a little kid," Jake grumbled.

"You are, sometimes," Chris muttered under his breath.

He couldn't locate his dad's electric shaver, but found a disposable one in the medicine cabinet. After running hot water into the sink and pulling a can of cheap shave cream out of the cabinet, he waited for his father to finish showering. When the water turned off, he handed him a towel through the gap between the curtain and scummy tiles. He was trying to leave his old man as much dignity and independence as he dared for the moment.

A minute later, his father stepped out of the tub with the towel knotted around his beer belly. His beard looked to be about three days old, and his hair was a snarled, damp, graying mess...but he had washed it. Chris could smell the spicy shampoo, a marvelous improvement over the body odor that had permeated every pore of the man before showering.

His father eyed the hot water in the sink and razor in Chris's hand. "I gotta shave, too?"

"Yup," Chris said. "This is the kind of lady you definitely shave for... and comb your hair. I'll go get you some clothes."

It took some doing, but he was able to locate a pair of passably clean slacks and an old dress shirt near the back of the bedroom closet. He also found some grayish but clean underwear in a bureau drawer, dark-colored socks and scuffed loafers. On his way back to the bathroom, he heard water running in the kitchen.

If Madelyn was making herself a cup of tea, she was braver than he. Long ago Chris had decided it wasn't safe to consume food or drink in his dad's home. A clean cup probably didn't exist in the place.

"Clothes, Dad!" he shouted through the door.

His father took them in, and Chris was gratified that he was looking better. Shaved, with his damp hair combed back from his booze-puffy face, he looked almost presentable. His eyes remained dreadfully bloodshot, but there was nothing to be done about that.

Chris changed the sheets on his dad's bed while he waited for him to dress. At last, Jake stepped from the bathroom.

"I really don't feel much like eating, kid," he said. "The old gut don't feel too hot this mornin'. Must be a touch of stomach flu."

"You'll feel better after you get something in your stomach," Chris assured him. "Come on. I want you to meet Madelyn."

His dad nodded obediently and followed him back through the living room and into the kitchen.

Chris stopped in shock at the kitchen doorway. While he'd been gone, Madelyn had bagged up all the trash and set it by the back door. She'd wiped down the table and countertops, and was nearly finished washing up the dishes.

"Looks like you've been pretty busy," Chris commented, amazed that she was tough enough to tackle the horrible mess. "Have trouble finding anything?"

"The dishwashing liquid. It was way under the sink, at the back." She set the last plate in the dish drainer and dried her hands on a paper towel.

"I'm sure it isn't used very often," Chris said wryly, then he gave Madelyn a conspiratorial wink. "Dad, this is Madelyn Phillips. She's the special friend I wanted you to meet."

Madelyn looked puzzled for a moment, then seemed to catch on. "I'm happy to meet you, Mr. McGuire," she said, stepping forward with her right hand extended as if this were their first meeting.

Jake's face lit up. "Aren't you a cute little thing?" he cooed, gripping her hand between his two paws instead of shaking it. "Not much like the girls Chris usually goes for!"

Chris shut his eyes, praying. There was no telling what his dad would say, since he had no concept of social tact.

"Oh, really," Madelyn said, sounding interested. "Have you met many of Chris's girlfriends?"

"Naw," Jake said sadly. "He never brings 'em over here. I don't think he's very proud of his old man."

"Dad, that's not—"

"Now, now," Jake interrupted, brushing Chris's objections aside, "it's the truth. I don't keep a very pretty house, and there isn't much to do around here since the cable's been turned off and..." He peered back into the living room. "Come to think of it, they repossessed the TV, too."

"Well, I'm pleased to meet you anyway," Madelyn said graciously. She glanced at Chris. "I'm awfully hungry. Do you think we could go now?"

Jake beat Chris to the door and swung it wide with a flourish, gesturing for Madelyn to go first. "Girl after my own heart. I'm starvin' myself. Let's move out, boy!"

At the Pancake House, Chris watched in awe as his father devoured a tall stack of blueberry flapjacks, soggy with maple syrup and surrounded by fat sausage links. He and Madelyn had each ordered waffles—she with strawberries on top, he with chopped pecans and maple syrup. Jake drank three cups of strong, black coffee with his meal. At last, he sat back from the table with a satisfied smile. Sticking his hands in the waist of his pants he observed his clean plate.

Madelyn giggled at him, as she continued working her way through her waffles. "I've never seen one person eat so much so quickly," she said. "You really must have been hungry, Mr. McGuire."

"Nothing like a hearty breakfast to start off the day," Jake chimed out, loosening his belt a notch. "So, how long you and my Chris been together?"

"We've known each other for about two months," Madelyn said, avoiding the issue of whether or not they still were or ever would be "together."

Jake looked at his son. "You treating her like a gentleman?"

"Of course, Dad." Chris smiled.

"Because if he's not, you come see me, young lady," Jake said solemnly. "He's not too old for a whippin' if he gets out of line. I brought my son up to be a gentleman."

Madelyn studied the older man, the smile leaving her lips. "I'm sure you did," she murmured.

"Sometimes had to whip the tar out of the boy. But you know what they say 'bout sparin' the rod."

She nodded solemnly, her eyes seeking out Chris's. He could see the beginnings of some sort of understanding there. Maybe she already sensed the physical as well as emotional abuse he'd suffered all those years back.

But now, Jake was on a roll. "His mother, she weren't one for touchin' a kid. 'Leave him alone!' she'd say. But I wasn't goin' to have no spoiled brat in my house. Chrissy, he learned young to obey the rules."

"Some rules are important," Madelyn allowed.

Jake smiled his most charming smile across the table at her. "I musta done a good job. He never once got into drugs, and after the time I caught him messin' round my liquor cabinet and wailed him good, he stayed away from the booze. Not good for a growin' kid, you know."

"I suspect not," she said, a tight edge to her voice.

"But there's only so much you can tell a boy once he gets to be a certain age. Kids think they know everything." Jake shook his head mournfully. "Chris took off soon as he graduated high school. Just left his old man clean."

"I hitched to New York City, thinking I'd latch on to a band there and make it big," Chris explained. "When that didn't work out, I headed for L.A. and did studio backup for some big-name groups, but I was never able to work my way into a regular spot with any of them."

Madelyn nodded, watching Chris's face intently, as if trying to discern the slightest twist of the facts. At last she turned back to Jake.

"But Chris came back home, so he must have cared about you, Mr. McGuire," she said gently.

Jake let out a sharp laugh. "Home? He ain't home 'cept when he has to come peel me off the couch or bring me some housekeepin' money. He wants his own place." He shot an annoyed glance at Chris, then poured himself a fourth cup of coffee from the carafe on the table. "Damned if I know why a kid would want to pay out good money for some crummy apartment in the city when he's got a perfectly good home in a nice neighborhood."

It was all Chris could do to stop himself from blurting out, *Because I can't live like you do—knee-deep in booze and excuses for a ruined life!* But he kept his mouth shut.

Madelyn glanced at Chris knowingly. "I guess by the time we get to be twenty-one, we want to feel independent... have our own places."

"Damned if it makes sense to me." Jake chuckled. "Hey, Chris, while I'm thinkin' 'bout it, got a little extra on you?" He winked. "Have to pay the maid this week."

They dropped Jake off at his house and Chris drove back toward the city.

"Seen enough?" he asked, his heart in his throat.

At least now Madelyn knew his childhood hadn't been a pretty one, filled with fairy tales read to him at bedtime, cookies and milk waiting for him when he returned from school.

He'd watched her standing in that filthy kitchen, and he'd thought how out of place she looked there. Her and her spotless white blouse and shining brown hair swept neatly back from her brow with a tortoiseshell headband. How she'd kept the disgust from showing in her face, he'd never know.

"No," she said calmly, "I want to see the rest of Chris McGuire...unless you'd prefer I pass judgment based solely on the last two hours."

A lightning bolt of horror shot through Chris's nerves. "No way!"

"Where to next?" she asked coolly.

He wished she'd move over closer to him on the truck's seat. She was practically hugging the passenger window.

"Band practice at Jimmy's house. He's our singer and writes most of our original pieces."

"Like the one you sang to me at the frat party?" she asked.

Chris winced as he pulled off the highway and down the ramp into the city. "I sort of improvised on that one."

Madelyn nodded and looked out the window for a long moment, as if she were thinking very hard. "Does Jimmy have a classical music background?"

Chris swallowed. Was she examining his friends, too? He hoped she wouldn't blame him for the way they acted, because he had a feeling they were heading for rough waters in the next couple of hours.

"No, Jimmy's never formally studied music. In fact he can only read a melody line, and that's how he writes it. The other guys in the band have to fill in their own parts. He plays a little guitar by ear."

"Oh," she said noncommittally. "I thought I caught part of a theme from Bach in the song you sang to me."

Chris smiled. "Jimmy wrote the lyrics—except for the Madelyn part—and started out with a standard ballad

backup. But he got stuck, so I took it and rewrote the melody borrowing from a Bach piece I'd learned in New York."

"Then you didn't make that up, about studying classical guitar?"

"No," he said. "But I only did it for a month. Then I didn't have any way of paying my teacher."

"I liked the song," she said, looking straight ahead at the road.

He turned to examine her expression, but her profile remained an unreadable blank. She's probably just being nice, he thought miserably. What the hell—he'd blown his chances with her already. But since he'd promised, he had to follow through with the rest of the day.

Twelve

Chris gave a perfunctory rap on Jimmy's basement door and walked in at the same moment his friend called out, "Yo!"

He led Madelyn by the hand into the dim, unfinished room. Jimmy was lounging on the sofa at the end of their makeshift studio. He looked up and scowled when he saw Madelyn.

"What's this?" he asked, getting to his feet.

"Someone I want you to meet," Chris said.

Steve came down the cellar stairs with a Pop-Tart in his hand and smiled shyly at Madelyn. "Hi! I remember you from the frat party. Weren't you the girl Chris took off after?"

"That's me," she admitted sheepishly.

"Didn't like our music, huh?" he teased.

She blushed. "It was...different. I've never been much into rock."

"That's cool," Steve said, laid back as always.

Jimmy moved in front of Chris, his hands braced on his hips. "Does this mean you're not staying for practice?" he demanded. "You know we got two gigs lined up for this weekend."

"I'm staying," Chris assured him. "I figured you wouldn't mind if Madelyn sat in." Chris turned to her. "This is Jimmy Moran. Jim, this is Madelyn Phillips."

Smiling, Madelyn stepped forward warily. "So you're the singer who's such a talented songwriter."

Jimmy looked thrown for a moment. "I write some stuff," he admitted, eyeing her skeptically.

"I could tell yours from the standard dance pieces you played and I've heard on my roommate's CDs. Your music sounds more interesting. Complex."

Jimmy shrugged, but Chris could tell by the softening in his eyes that he was pleased with her compliment.

"So, where'd you meet Chris?" he asked.

Chris held his breath. This was one of the moments he'd most dreaded.

"In English class," she stated casually.

"*English* class?" he repeated incredulously. "As in *school?*"

"As in college," Chris said. "I started going part-time to the University of Chicago last month. I'm taking six credits in liberal arts."

"You go to college?" Jimmy repeated, scowling.

Chris nodded.

Steve polished off his pastry and licked his fingers clean. "What you gonna be, a doctor or something?"

"No, probably a social worker. But it'll take a long time for me to earn enough credits, just for an associate's degree."

Jimmy's upper lip curled in the sneer Chris had anticipated. "What do you think, you're *better* than us? You think you got some kind of megabrain? Like we're stupid or something?" he shouted.

"No," Chris said firmly. "I just want to see if I can help out kids in families like mine."

"So you've been stringing me along!" he spat out. "Telling me you were coming back to the band, that you were serious about our music."

Chris reached out to touch his shoulder, but the singer pulled away with a vicious jerk.

"It's not like that, Jimmy. Cool down. I just want to try and see if I can handle college. If this semester goes okay, I'll take a few more courses and still have time for the band." Chris hesitated, then put into words what he'd been mulling over for months. "Hey, man, we can't play music all our lives."

Jimmy glared at him, then at Madelyn, as if she were to blame for his guitarist's treachery. He spun around, cursing bitterly under his breath, and bolted up the cellar stairs. The door at the top slammed shut.

For a long moment no one spoke. Then Steve sat down at his drums, picked up the sticks and smacked the cymbals. "So much for practice," he muttered as they rang ominously.

Chris shook his head. "I was afraid of this. I figured he'd feel threatened by my going to school."

"He'll cool down," Steve said, "eventually. It'll just take him a while to get used to the idea. You two have been together for a long time."

"Yeah," Chris said sadly, remembering their high school days. He and Jimmy had been inseparable. There were the many nights his old man had kicked him out of the house; Jimmy's door had always been open.

Madelyn cleared her throat. "Maybe we should go," she said timidly, glancing toward the dark stairway.

"I guess," Chris agreed.

"Chill a few minutes," Steve suggested. "You and me can at least go over our parts on the new numbers. Paul and Kurt will be here in an hour, but I guess they won't want to work unless Jimmy's in the mood."

Chris turned to Madelyn. "Do you mind staying a little longer?"

"No," she said, smiling softly at him. "Go ahead and work. I'll just sit over here and listen." She walked over to

the sagging couch and sat down, pulling her knees up and curling her legs around her.

Chris smiled encouragingly at her, thinking she must be incredibly nervous. Jimmy's temper wasn't a pretty sight.

Chris took his guitar out of its case, hooked into the amps and tuned up. "Let's take it from the top of 'Raging On,'" he suggested.

"You got it," Steve said.

The song started out with an instrumental section then segued into a vocal that Jimmy would have sung if he'd been there. Without thinking much about what he was doing, Chris started singing the rough, rocking lyrics. It was an angry, emotional song—the kind Jimmy, with his low, scratchy voice, performed well.

Chris did his best to sound tough and angry with the world. He glanced over at Madelyn. Her eyes sparkled, and she held a graceful hand over her mouth, looking as if she were struggling to keep from laughing. He broke up.

"Hey, cut it out!" He laughed so hard, he had to wipe tears out of his eyes. "This is serious stuff."

"I can see that," she managed, then couldn't stop from laughing herself.

"I was okay, wasn't I?" he asked Steve.

"Well, let's just say you do better on ballads. Maybe Jimmy will write you another love song someday."

"Fat chance," Chris said, shaking his head.

"I might," a voice whispered from the top of the stairs.

Chris stared up at his friend. "I thought you'd washed your hands of me."

"I couldn't sit up there and listen to you make a damn farce of one of my best songs," Jimmy grumbled. He started down the stairs. "Thanks for stopping him," he muttered at Madelyn.

She blinked, as if unsure how to respond. "You're welcome," she said softly.

Jimmy picked up a mike. "Take it from the intro of the first verse," he said.

When Jimmy sang, his voice took on a remorseless fury that Steve responded to on his drums. Chris played the lead guitar part, keeping up with Jimmy's nods to pick up the pace, until they were racing through the song like a runaway train.

When they'd finished, all three musicians were breathless and they looked at each other, waiting for someone to say it was as good as they'd thought it had been.

Out of the silence came the sound of Madelyn clapping her hands. "That was wonderful... really exciting!" she cried, jumping up from the couch, forgetting her shyness. "I wish you'd played that at the frat house. They'd have *loved* it!"

Jimmy looked at her hard, and Chris was afraid he was about to cut her down. He stepped forward to distract his explosive friend.

"She's not used to our kind of music..." he began in an apologetic tone.

"No!" Jimmy snapped, studying her with new interest. "She's not a musician—that's cool. If she reacts to 'Raging' like that, people who just go to parties to dance will like it, too." He turned to her again. "You got time to hang around?"

"I guess... sure," she said hesitantly.

"Good. Soon as the other guys get here, we'll run through the whole new set. You tell us the songs you like and the ones that stink."

"I think I can handle that," she said with a smile.

Her eyes drifted over to meet Chris's. He still couldn't tell what she was thinking, but at least she was still with him.

It was nearly one in the afternoon before they left Jimmy's house, and they hadn't had lunch. Jimmy dropped

them off at the nearest Metra stop, and they took the subway back into the city.

As the truck screeched and jolted along the rails, Chris struggled with his warring emotions. He was dying to know what Madelyn thought of the hours they'd spent with the band. Having an audience, the guys hadn't messed around as much as they usually did during a practice. It seemed more like an audition, and they'd played seriously, producing what Chris thought was a great sound.

Madelyn had given her stamp of approval to three songs that she'd especially liked. She thought most were just okay. She'd hated two and had been very blunt with Jimmy about them, giving her reasons. He'd listened with uncharacteristic patience and hadn't objected to her gentle criticism.

"I sort of figured those two needed more work," he muttered thoughtfully when she'd finished speaking. He looked at Chris. "Let's pull 'em from the set until I have more time to fix them."

The Metra jerked to a halt, and Chris took Madelyn's arm as they exited through the sliding doors. "There's a McDonald's just around the corner from here," he suggested.

"Good, I'm famished."

"You haven't said much since we left Jimmy's," Chris commented a few minutes later as they sat down at a table near a window where they could warm up in the sunshine.

"I've been thinking, that's all." She bit enthusiastically into her Big Mac.

"About the music? Must sound pretty weird to you."

"No, actually the more I listen to your songs, the better I like them. I think that learning to appreciate any kind of music takes some time. It was something else."

"What?" Chris asked, eaten up with curiosity. He longed for some assurance that she wasn't going to walk away from him ten minutes from now.

Madelyn shrugged and popped a few fries into her mouth. "I was thinking that you were pretty brave to register for classes at the university. You knew that your friends would react the way they did. Didn't you?"

"Of course I knew," he admitted. "I might have started school a year ago when I came back to Chicago if I hadn't been scared that everyone I knew would cut me off. But Jimmy and Steve are good guys. Just like it will take you a while to get used to my music, I guess it's going to take them a while to accept the scholastic side of my life."

She nodded, but didn't respond to his hint that she might eventually accept him. "Where to next?" she asked in a businesslike voice.

Chris stared at her across the table. Why did she have to be so damned stubborn about this? If she thought he was okay, why not just tell him? On the other hand, if she had already made up her mind that he wasn't her kind of person, he guessed he'd rather she put off telling him.

If this was to be their last day together, he wanted to stretch it out as long as possible. "Razzles," he said. "We'll go there next."

She wrinkled up her nose, looking perplexed. "Razzles? What's that?"

"It's where I really work. I told you I waited tables at a posh restaurant called Ramone's because I didn't think you'd be impressed by my real job. I tend bar at a dance club in the Loop."

"I see," she murmured, looking away from him.

"Listen," he said tightly, capturing her chin between his thumb and index finger and forcing her to look into his eyes. "Yeah, it was another lie. But you already suspected that. You'd asked around about Ramone's and guessed it didn't exist. But that doesn't matter."

"It doesn't?" she asked stiffly. Her eyes sparked with her own defiance.

"No, it doesn't. The important thing is, I'm not ashamed that I serve drinks in a bar. If that's what I have to do to support myself and get up some cash for tuition, I'll do it. And I'll keep on as long as it takes me to get my degree."

Madelyn arched a brow at him. "You will, will you?"

"Yes," he said, feeling sure of what he was doing for the first time.

"Then you don't need my approval, do you?" she asked, her voice suddenly quiet.

"No." His hand dropped away from her chin, and he sat back on the bench to better observe her gentle smile. "No, I guess I don't. But it would sure make me happy if you were with me for the trip."

She bit her lower lip and looked away, across the crowded restaurant. "Let's go see this Razzles place."

They reached the bar in the Loop a little before three o'clock, in plenty of time to set up for the early Happy Hour crowd. Chris used his key to let himself in, knowing Gary would probably be in his office, in the back.

As he motioned Madelyn through the door ahead of him, she scanned the place. It was a far cry from her usual hangouts like the Art Institute, with their tastefully lit portraits and landscapes and rich wood floors. There, the atmosphere demanded, "Don't touch *a thing!* We're valuable. And don't even think of talking above a whisper!"

Here, the atmosphere was electric—or would be once the lights flickered on and the place was packed with young professionals and students from Chicago's Loop.

"It's quiet now, but it'll be deafening in here by six o'clock," he warned.

Madelyn nodded, her eyes wide as she walked across the floor and gingerly perched on a stool at the bar. It occurred to him that he'd been right weeks ago, when he'd thought how out-of-place she'd be in Razzles. This must look like another planet to a girl like her.

"Madelyn, if you don't want to stay—"

She waved a hand. "Don't be silly. I'm fine," she said in a quiet voice.

"You're sure?" He sat down on the stool beside her, absorbing from a painful distance the peacefulness and subtle beauty he'd once held close. Even now he ached to enfold her sweet body in his arms.

She smiled up at him. "Where do you stand? Back there?" she asked, pointing to the other side of the bar.

"Right there. I work the whole bar by myself most nights. Weekends Gary comes out front to lend a hand. He has a part-timer who fills in on nights when I can't be here."

She pursed her lips and stared pensively at the wall of liquor bottles rising up behind the bar.

"Must seem like a pretty strange way to make a living to you, I guess. You don't drink hardly at all. And my dad being the way he is..."

Sometimes it didn't make sense to him, either. He was probably feeding drinks to some guy in his twenties who would someday end up like his old man.

"I don't know," she said softly, running her fingertips across the polished chrome surface. "Like you said, it's just a job. You do it because the pay covers your tuition and rent. I don't think you can be responsible for everyone you serve."

"Yeah, I guess." Still, it did bother him some nights.

Madelyn sighed. "I waited on tables at a Pizza Hut last summer. I guess it's sort of like that."

"You mean you contributed to the obesity of your hometown, like I encouraged drinking?"

She grinned at him for the first time that day. "No, silly. I mean, I don't expect to be serving up pizza for a career. But if that's what it takes to get me through college, I'll do it," she announced through gritted teeth.

There was a fierceness in her voice he'd never heard before, a determination to make her life turn out as she dreamed it could. He loved her all the more because of her intensity, and his heart ached when he realized how much alike they were in so many ways...yet they were likely to go their separate ways after today.

He tentatively reached out and touched the backs of her velvety fingers, curled up on the bar. It seemed as if it had been years since he'd felt her skin beneath his. His heart stopped for the few seconds his fingertips hovered over her hand. She could pull away at any moment, yet her hand was miraculously still pressed against the slick, silvery surface when his covered hers.

She was warm and soft. Chris closed his eyes, remembering how her body had felt as it lazily smoothed across his naked chest while they lay in bed after making love.

Dear God, what he wouldn't give to be with her like that again!

Slowly he stroked the back of her hand with his thumb, watching the motion, hearing her breathing deepen at his touch.

"I fell in love with you the first time I saw you in that lecture hall," he whispered.

"I know," she said.

"I took one look at you and I thought, 'I could never get a girl that classy and sophisticated to like me.'"

Madelyn looked up at him, her brown eyes huge and glassy. She said nothing, so he went on.

"I said to myself, 'You're the town drunk's kid. You always have been, and nothing much has changed since you were in grade school. You don't have any money. The only home you've ever known is a filthy matchbox in a blue-collar neighborhood that's going downhill. You aren't even taking a serious credit load at U. of C. What do you have to impress her with?'"

"And how did you answer yourself?" she asked.

He shook his head dismally. "When I found out you loved classical music, I couldn't admit I'd played rock all my life and didn't know Beethoven from... from..."

"Schubert?" she supplied.

"Whatever," he grumbled. "And pouring drinks at a bar is as blue collar as you can get. I had nothing... nothing to interest you... and you let me know that the first couple of times we met in class."

Madelyn winced. "I didn't know you then. You were so different from any other guy I'd ever met, Chris." She laughed sadly, shaking her head. "If Sandy had told me four months ago that I'd be dating a guy who wore a black leather jacket and an earring, I'd have had her committed."

"Yeah," Chris muttered. "I guess it must have been a shock that someone like me would even try to pick up a girl like you."

"Yes," she said, looking him in the eye. "It was a shock."

His heart shattered into a million pieces inside his chest. *Here it comes,* he thought miserably, *she's going to tell me to take the long hike.*

Chris lifted his hand away reluctantly and turned on the bar stool, dropping his forehead against his fists. "Shit," he groaned.

"Chris, listen to me," Madelyn said, touching him on the shoulder.

He pulled away, anger building out of his pain. "Forget it! You don't have to be nice to me. Just say it! Say you don't want anything to do with me!"

"No!" she shouted, her eyes suddenly bright with her own fury. "No! I won't just tell you goodbye! You're going to listen to me, Christopher McGuire, because you haven't heard a word I've said."

"Oh, right!" He laughed wildly, shooting up off the stool. "Like I didn't hear you at the dorm when you said you never wanted to see me again!"

"Damn you, let me explain!" she shouted back at him.

He was amazed that she'd actually sworn at him. "Fine. You have five minutes. Then I have to get to work." He sat down again, bracing himself for her list of reasons she couldn't stay with him.

Madelyn cleared her throat and looked him straight in the eyes. "I admitted I was shocked that someone like you would try to pick up a girl like me. That's true. I couldn't believe a guy as cool as Chris McGuire would honestly care a fig for a boring, plain-Jane like me...."

She pressed her fingertips over his lips when he opened his mouth to object.

"It's my turn, remember?" He nodded, and she went on. "You were so different from any other boy who'd shown any interest in me. They were all quiet and bookish, like me—nice but boring. One played the clarinet in the school orchestra. That's about as musical as any of them got. They all went to summer camps—computer or scholastic types, not sports. They all made honors every semester in high school. And every one of them went straight on to college, paid for by his parents."

Chris looked at her, unsure where she was headed.

"Then you came along, and I was sure you were playing some sort of practical joke on me. Maybe you got a kick out of picking the homeliest girl in the class, sitting next to her, then coming on to her, just to see her make a fool of herself when she thought you liked her."

"I'm not like that!" Chris objected.

"I know...now," she said. "But when we first met, I had no idea who or what you were."

"Then I started feeding you a bunch of lies," Chris pointed out, shaking his head. He was beginning to under-

stand Madelyn's early timidity around him. It wasn't snobbishness that kept her from warming up to him. It was fear.

"Right. You told me all that stuff about studying classical guitar, pretended you liked Impressionist art, then wove these fantastic stories about your childhood and another about where you worked."

"I was just trying to make you like me!" Chris pleaded.

"You still don't understand, do you?" Madelyn demanded, shoving him hard in the chest.

He slipped off the side of the stool and saved himself from falling with one foot. Chris blinked at her, startled by her fierce temper.

"Of course I understand!" he retorted. "I didn't push the right buttons, so you're going to dump me!"

"No! No! No!" Madelyn screamed. "I was going to dump you because I'd cared about you. I'd started to fall in love with you, and we slept together, and I'd trusted you—then I found out you'd lied to me about almost everything in your life!"

He stared at her. "You mean, it was *the fact* I'd lied, not who I am that turned you off?"

She rolled her eyes. "Finally, the man gets it!"

Chris risked a weak smile. "Hey, wait a minute. You just said something about, you *were going to* dump me... Does that mean that you... that we..." He didn't dare put his hopes into words.

"It means I love you, Chris. It means it doesn't matter whether we always have the same tastes in music, or dress the same, or whether or not our fathers abused us by beating us or by ignoring us.... None of that matters."

"What about school? I'm taking two lousy courses."

"So it'll take you longer to finish than it'll take me," Madelyn stated. "The arithmetic is pretty simple."

"And Razzles?"

She looked around. "I'll have to see what it's like at night with a crowd in it. I don't think I'll ever be much of a barfly. But I guess it's not so different from any other place where people get together—like a club or church hall. So Razzles serves drinks and supplies dance music. It's a lot nicer than that frat house basement."

He stared at her in mounting amazement, then reached out and gripped her shoulders. "Are you saying we can be together again as long as I tell you the truth? That's all I have to do? I can still be me?"

She laughed at him, her eyes sparkling with tears of happiness. "Chris, that's all I've ever wanted. I just need to know the real you. What there was of you that I really saw was exciting, fun and loving."

Chris pulled her into his arms and held on to her, feeling her warmth, cherishing the emotional quiver in her body. Then he turned his head and crooked a finger under her chin to brush his lips across hers. He kissed her hungrily. As he felt her melt in his arms, his kiss deepened and he was blissfully lost in her softness.

Gradually, he became aware of her poking him in the shoulder blade, then pounding frantically with her fist on his back.

He pulled away to look down at her with concern. Her eyes were enormous. She stared at something behind him.

Chris spun around.

Gary stood in his office doorway, an enormous grin stretching across his face. "Gee, and I thought I was paying you to come in early and slice lemons...."

Chris laughed, embarrassed more for Madelyn than for himself. "I want you to meet someone very special, Gar."

Madelyn blushed shyly. "Hi, I'm Chris's friend, Madelyn Phillips. If you'd like, I can leave and come back later."

Gary looked solemnly from her to Chris and back again. "If you know how to slice lemons you can stay."

* * *

That night when Razzles closed, Madelyn followed Chris outside and waited on the sidewalk while he locked up. He'd been so busy they hadn't had any time alone together. But she didn't mind. The lively bar was crammed with exciting young people. Although she hadn't danced, it was a great place for people-watching.

"I like your bar," she said softly as he turned to face her.

He kissed her happily on the mouth and flung a long arm around her shoulders. "Good. I hope you'll drop by some nights when I'm working. I like having you here."

She smiled up at him, then drew her shoulders up in an exaggerated shiver. "It's awfully cold tonight, don't you think?"

He lifted his face into the stiff wind off Lake Michigan. "Not that bad for this time of year," he commented.

"Isn't your apartment pretty close to here?" she asked.

"Yeah, just a few blocks. Why?"

"Oh," she said, not daring to look him in the eye, "I was just thinking that I didn't want to walk all the way back to campus in this cold."

It took him only a second to catch on. "And the Metra this time of night might be dangerous."

"Unless you came with me, but that's a lot of trouble for you to come all the way to campus and back. You must be awfully tired," she said sympathetically.

"Exhausted," he agreed, taking her in his arms on the dark sidewalk. He kissed her lightly on the nose, on the forehead, then dropped his lips to taste hers. "Want to bunk at my place tonight?"

Madelyn nodded, suddenly feeling bashful, as if they'd never made love before. Then she envisioned Chris—lifting his shirt over his head, revealing his smooth, muscled chest...then crossing the room to unbutton her blouse. She could almost feel his hands on her body, soothing her,

making love to her in all the many glorious ways she'd hungered for during their weeks of separation.

"You're sure?" he asked solemnly. "I don't think I could leave you alone if we were together tonight."

"I'd be disappointed if you did," she whispered breathlessly into his ear. "Let's go home to bed, Chris."

Thirteen

Madelyn felt herself floating slowly to the surface of her consciousness through layers of blissfully warm sleep. She sighed, opening her eyes a sliver, not wanting to break the spell. The room was black, except for a faint predawn glow filtering through the blinds. It took her a moment to remember where she was and why she felt so happy. Then she sensed Chris's body lying beside her in the sheets, and she knew.

Smiling into the dark she whispered, "Right where I want to be, that's where I am."

"Wha-? You okay?" a sleep-gruff voice asked.

"I'm fine, just perfect," she murmured, sliding back into Chris's arms.

She shifted around so that her rump nestled cozily into the furry nest of his masculinity and her spine was protectively curled against his strong chest. Laying her cheek on his biceps, she drew his top arm around her like a human cloak.

Never had she felt so right with a boy.... No, she corrected herself, *with a man!* The others had been schoolboys, clumsy experiments on the way to the real thing. Chris was without question a man, and a person she could trust and depend upon.

With a contented sigh, she wiggled her bottom...and felt an answering response as Chris rapidly hardened.

"Oh?" she murmured, as her own desires swelled, filling her limbs with an almost irresistible need to wrap themselves around Chris's muscled torso and draw him once

again into her...although they'd only finished making love a few hours earlier. "Chris, are you...are you awake?"

"Mmm-hmm."

"You aren't thinking about—"

"Are you?"

Her cheek blazed against the cool skin of his arm. "I...well, I was actually thinking about what we did just before we fell asleep."

"And?"

She laughed out loud. "What do you want, a report card?"

He lifted his arm so that he could reach her breasts and trace lazy circles around each nipple with the tip of one finger. "It doesn't have to be *A, B* or *C*," he said, his lips brushing the sensitive lobe of her ear. "A general indication of your pleasure will be satisfactory."

Madelyn grinned at his playful tone. She took a deep breath, steadying herself so she wouldn't crack up when she delivered the next line.

"I, um, I'm not sure."

"What?" he gasped, shooting up onto one elbow and dumping her into the pillow.

There was enough light in the room for her to make out the faint shape of his head and shoulders looming over her. She didn't know if he could see her expression or not, but she managed to keep a straight face anyway.

"Well, it's so difficult to know. I mean, I thought it was pretty good, but I could be wrong. Perhaps," she said slowly, "what we need is a test case."

She could feel him staring down at her, as he tried to figure out if she was kidding or serious.

"A test case," he repeated. "Like, we should make love again?"

"All over again, start to finish."

"The exact same way?"

"Not necessarily. Only your best work will do, though, since this is a judged event."

"Right now?" he growled sexily, flexing this muscled arms to drop down and gnaw voraciously at her throat. He took his full weight on one arm, then smoothed up along her thigh to her hip with his free hand.

"The judge is ready," she managed to get out, before bursting into giggles, unable any longer to play the straight man.

In the next second, she was totally serious. Madelyn gazed up at Chris, feeling her hunger for him build to a white-hot flame. Her arms ached for him. Her soul thirsted for what only he could give her—the other half of her identity.

"I love you, Chris. Make love to me, please."

"My pleasure," he murmured.

And their pleasures blazed through a myriad of fiery sensations both erotic and tender, until they lay gasping in spent passion and delirious with ecstacy within each other's arms.

The Razzles' Sunday crowd was made up of locals from the Loop, come to watch pro football games on the big-screen TV. However, the Bears weren't playing that day, and so there was an even smaller crowd than usual.

It was Chris's day off, but he couldn't stop himself from diving behind the bar to pour glasses of wine for each of the girls. He'd invited Jessica, Becky and C.J. down for a drink so that they could meet Madelyn.

When he returned with four glasses and a beer for himself on the tray, he was horrified to hear C.J. jabbering on to Madelyn as if they'd been best friends for years.

"Yeah, he really does have a nice apartment now.... But, boy, you should have seen it... well, it took the four of us hours to clear away that clutter and—"

"C.J.!" he gasped, fixing her with a horrified stare. "What have you been telling my lady while I was gone?"

"Everything under the sun," Jessica said lightly, buffing her nails on her sweater sleeve.

Becky giggled. "I think she wants to make sure you've left nothing unsaid."

Madelyn laughed, looking delighted with the other girls. He was glad they were getting along, but felt a little outnumbered.

"Everyone deserves to be able to keep a few secrets," she murmured. "There are a few things of a personal nature that I wouldn't want anyone to know."

"Is that so?" Chris said, his interest piqued.

"Never mind asking, because I wouldn't tell you if you tugged out every one of my fingernails."

C.J. meekly picked up her glass from the tray and sipped. "You don't have to worry about me. I'm the epitome of discretion," she announced, raising her glass.

Chris laughed. How could he be angry with her when Madelyn sat beside him? He reached out and took her tiny hand beneath the table. Her cheeks glowed with the healthy color of love.

"Oh, I almost forgot," Madelyn said, pulling her hand away after a soft little squeeze to let him know she wouldn't be out of his reach for long. "I have something for you."

She dug around in her purse for several seconds before pulling out a slip of blue notepaper.

"What's this?" he asked. "Miriam Storm... 1400 Lake Shore Drive, number 705?"

Jessica twisted in her seat to read the slip in Chris's hand. "There's a phone number, too." She glared suspiciously at him. "I hope this isn't one of your old flames trying to get in touch."

"Of course not," he groaned. "I wouldn't have any way of meeting someone from a posh address like this." He

stared at Madelyn, genuinely puzzled. "What's this all about?"

"That's my roommate's mother. Her mom is planning a fiftieth birthday party for her dad, and she's hiring entertainment. Like a magician, stand-up comedian, a band and a pianist to play Harry Connick, Jr. type of background music. There are supposed to be around a hundred guests."

Chris couldn't see the connection between him and a private party for people the age of his old man. "So?"

"So, Sandy mentioned your band to her mom. She'd been looking for a local band that played a lot of alternative rock, since that's her husband's latest passion. Seems he was into country and Garth Brooks last year, and now he's collecting old U2 and R.E.M. albums." Madelyn paused and smiled at him. "Mrs. Storm would like you to give her a call."

Chris stared at her in disbelief. In the back of his mind, a thousand possibilities were exploding like fireworks. "Do you have any idea what this might mean?" he asked.

"Another job for the band?" she asked.

"More than that." He took two swift chugs of his beer. "With a hundred upper-class professionals in the crowd, we'd stand a good chance of running into *someone* with connections."

"Oh, I don't know...." she began warily.

Chris laughed, feeling as giddy as a little kid in an amusement park. "I don't mean some guy with a cigar is going to walk up and say, 'Hey, kid, sign this recording contract. I'm gonna make you a star.' But still, you never know." He bounced on his chair, he was so excited. "That's the fluky way these things happen."

Madelyn grinned at him. "You sound like Jimmy."

"Nah, I know it's a long shot. But we're good and getting better every day... and all it will take is a little luck to

get us started." He threw his arms around her and hugged her so hard, she squeaked in protest.

It wasn't so much the hope of making it big in music that thrilled him. He could get just as excited about holding his degree in his hand and knowing he was going to do some good in his city. No, it was more than that. It was Madelyn's gesture, her presenting him with this chance that told him she accepted not only his music, she accepted *him*.

She wasn't passing judgment on his future, demanding that he get a degree and land a respectable nine-to-five job. She wasn't trying to make him into something different from what he was. She was telling him, *It's okay to be Chris McGuire...play your music...not like Picasso...make fun of avant-garde sculptures. I don't care! Just be yourself, and I'll love you.*

"You're wonderful," he muttered happily into her ear. Then he ignored the other three girls at the table and kissed his Madelyn soundly on the lips.

* * * * *

Next month: Becky meets her match in

Getting Personal: Becky

by Janet Quin-Harkin

One

Becky was amazed by the clues she could pick up from personal ads. She believed she could sense a person's whole personality from the way he or she phrased an ad...or from his or her name.

Take for example a name like Michael Max. That was the most intriguing name she had ever heard. What sort of person was called Michael Max? A movie star, an artist... certainly not someone who worked for a bank or a supermarket.

Besides, his voice didn't sound as if he were ordinary. It had been a wonderful voice—a deep, gravelly, haunting, *sexy* voice that had made her heart beat faster even before he gave his name or told Becky the wording of his ad.

She heard the voice now again, echoing through her head: "The name's Michael. Michael Max. Have you got that?"

Becky trembled again at the effect those simple words had on her. Was it possible to conjure up a person in your mind, just from the sound of his voice? She had him pictured perfectly by now—tall and dark-haired, and he'd have arresting blue eyes that would make her melt when he looked at her....

Becky started at the sound of a horn and leapt back onto the sidewalk as a taxi took the corner at high speed, missing her by inches. That was the problem with daydreaming—once she started fantasizing, she was completely lost to the real world.

"Get your act together, Becky Delaney," she told herself severely, "and forget about Michael Max. You aren't going to meet him, so that's that. And even if you did meet him, you know that he wouldn't be interested in you. So concentrate on the important things, like getting to the office on time and in one piece!"

She was breathless and her cheeks were stinging from the cold wind by the time she reached work at *Chicago Now*. Her hands were cold, too, and she wondered how much longer she could go on walking to work. If snow came early this year, as predicted, she'd have to give it up and take the bus. Then she'd have no more chance to save money until spring.

"Well, don't you look the picture of health," her co-worker Mary greeted her as Becky stepped into the cubicle they shared.

"These rosy cheeks are totally numb with cold," Becky said. "The wind was bitter out there today. I don't know how much longer I can keep walking to work."

"All winter, as long as you don't mind frostbite," Mary said. "You want me to get you a cup of coffee? I was on my way to the boss's office and I planned to sneak myself a cup as I passed."

"I'd love one, thanks," Becky said.

"Just take any calls if any come in," Mary said.

"Don't worry," Becky said. "The sort of people who place our ads don't get up before ten o'clock."

"Unless some of them haven't been to bed all night," Mary said, chuckling. "I'll be right back."

Becky watched her fondly as she walked elegantly away. Everything Mary did was elegant, from the way she spoke with her low, smooth voice, to the way she draped her long, African-print scarf around her head when she went out. Becky was glad that she and Mary shared a cubicle. From

the very beginning she had made the big city and the new job less frightening for Becky.

Mary was a tall African-American woman in her thirties, supporting two children alone. She had once been a nightclub singer but now she needed a day job while the children were in school. Becky had been a little intimidated by Mary at first. But after a few days she found that Mary and she shared the same sense of humor and that Mary was rapidly becoming a second mother to her.

"Here. Drink that while it's hot," Mary said, returning with a large, steaming mug. "And don't go near the boss today if you can help it. He must have had a disappointing night last night because he is in the mother of bad moods. I asked him if I could leave early on Thursday to go to my kids' school concert and he said sure, if I wanted to look for another job while I was out."

"Mary, that's ridiculous," Becky exclaimed. "I could handle your work for one afternoon, and it's important to your kids that you go to their concerts."

"I know," Mary said, "but Stan doesn't feel the same way. I suppose it's because the accountant was by yesterday and the figures were worse than ever. We're losing money no matter what we do."

"I don't see how that's our fault," Becky said. "We just take down ads when we have a caller."

"Maybe the whole of greater Chicago is already paired up except us," Mary said. "Which reminds me. You didn't go to that place again last night, did you?"

"What place?" Becky asked innocently.

"You know very well what place—Razzles."

Becky looked away as she nodded yes.

"Becky!" Mary exclaimed. "And after all those words of wisdom from your aunt Mary, too. As my old grandmother used to say, 'You'll be the death of me, child!'"

Becky had to smile. "It's okay, Mary," she said. "Nothing has happened. He hasn't even shown up yet."

"And how do you know that?"

"Because I'd know him if I saw him."

"How would you know? He didn't give you a description, did he?"

Becky grinned nervously. "No, he didn't give me any description. I just... know what he must look like from the sound of his voice."

"He might be forty-five, fat and balding."

Becky shook her head. "Oh, no. He had a young, sexy voice. He was thirty at the oldest."

"Do you know how many radio announcers have young, sexy voices and are really old and bald?" Mary asked. "A voice is nothing to go on. And the sooner you learn that, the better...."

Is the future what it's cracked up to be?

This November, discover the bright lights of the big city with Becky in

GETTING PERSONAL: BECKY
by Janet Quin-Harkin

A small-town girl, she came to the big city seeking fame and fortune...and ended up taking personal ads over the phone for the local "alternative" paper. Life seemed pretty boring until she started following a cute mystery man named Michael. What made a guy like him desperate enough to take out a personal ad? Bursting with curiosity, she waited and watched—until *he* caught *her*.

The ups and downs of life as you know it continue with

GETTING ATTACHED: CJ
by Wendy Corsi Staub (December)

GETTING A LIFE: MARISSA
by Kathryn Jensen (January)

Get smart. Get into "The Loop"!

Only from Silhouette®

where passion lives.

LOOP4

Celebrate Halloween with Silhouette's newest romance series,

Spine-tingling romances from the dark side.

In October, enjoy these Silhouette Shadows titles:

SS #41 MEMORY'S LAMP
by Marilyn Tracy

Sandy Rush's mind is no longer her own, as a murder victim's every memory becomes Sandy's experience. And when sexy Cliff Broderick begins to show up in her recollections, Sandy is left reeling with doubt about Cliff's ulterior motives—not to mention the desire erupting between them.

SS #42 BETWEEN DUSK AND DAWN
by Val Daniels
Premiere

Jonna Sanders peaceful world had erupted into a living nightmare. Eerie phone calls in the dead of night, unseen intruders—and mysterious, yet sensuous, stranger Sam Barton. Was Sam's love to be trusted—or battled with?

Don't miss these chilling, thrilling love stories... from Silhouette Shadows.

Available in October at a store near you.

Dark secrets, dangerous desire...

Lovers DARK AND DANGEROUS

Three spine-tingling tales from the dark side of love.

This October, enter the world of shadowy romance as Silhouette presents the third in their annual tradition of thrilling love stories and chilling story lines. Written by three of Silhouette's top names:

**LINDSAY McKENNA
LEE KARR
RACHEL LEE**

Haunting a store near you this October.

Only from

Silhouette®

...where passion lives.

LDD

Award-winning author

BARBARA BRETTON

Dares you to take a trip through time this November with

Tomorrow & Always

How fast can an eighteenth-century man torn with duty and heartache run? Will he find the freedom and passion he craves in another century? Do the arms of a woman from another time hold the secret to happiness? And can the power of their love defeat the mysterious forces that threaten to tear them apart?

...Stay tuned.

And you thought loving a man from the twentieth century was tough.

Reach for the brightest star in women's fiction with

MBBTA

THE LOOP FREE SHOPPING SPREE SWEEPSTAKES
OFFICIAL RULES—NO PURCHASE NECESSARY

To enter, hand-print on a 3"x5" card the words "THE LOOP FREE SHOPPING SPREE," your name and address, and mail to: The Loop Free Shopping Spree Sweepstakes, 3010 Walden Ave., P.O. Box 9069, Buffalo, NY 14269-9069, or P.O. Box 638, Fort Erie, Ontario, L2A 5X3. Limit: one entry per envelope. Entries must be sent via First Class mail and be received no later than 12/30/94. No liability is assumed for lost, late or misdirected mail.

One prize, that of a 3-day/2-night, weekend (Saturday night stay required) trip for 2 (at least one traveler must be 21 years of age or older) to Chicago, Illinois, or at winner's option, $2,000 cash, will be awarded in a random drawing (to be conducted no later than 2/15/95) from amongst all eligible entries received. Trip includes round-trip air transportation from commercial airport nearest winner's residence, accommodations at the Chicago Omni and $500 cash for a shopping spree. Approximate trip value, which will vary dependent upon winner's residence and time of year travel occurs: $2,500. Winner selection is under the supervision of D.L. Blair, Inc., an independent judging organization, whose decisions are final. Travelers (and parent/guardian of a minor) must sign and return a release of liability prior to traveling. Trip must be taken by 3/15/96 and is subject to airline schedules and accommodations availability. Prizes are valued in U.S. dollars.

Sweepstakes offer is open to residents of the U.S. (except Puerto Rico) and Canada, except employees and immediate family members of Harlequin Enterprises, Ltd., its affiliates, subsidiaries, and all agencies, entities or persons connected with the use, marketing or conduct of this sweepstakes. All federal, state, provincial, municipal and local laws apply.

Offer void wherever prohibited by law. Taxes and/or duties are the sole responsibility of the winners. Any litigation within the Province of Quebec respecting the conduct and awarding of prize may be submitted to the Regie des loteries et courses du Quebec. Prize will be awarded; winner will be notified by mail. No substitution of prize is permitted. Odds of winning are dependent upon the number of eligible entries received.

Potential winner must sign and return an Affidavit of Eligibility within 30 days of notification. In the event of noncompliance within this time period, prize may be awarded to an alternate winner. Prize notification returned as undeliverable may result in the awarding of prize to an alternate winner. By acceptance of their prize, winner consents to use of their name, photograph or likeness for purposes of advertising, trade and promotion on behalf of Harlequin Enterprises, Ltd., without further compensation, unless prohibited by law. A Canadian winner must correctly answer an arithmetical skill-testing question in order to be awarded the prize.

For the name of the winner, (available after 3/15/95) send a separate stamped, self-addressed envelope to: The Loop Free Shopping Spree Sweepstakes, 3124 Winner, P.O. Box 4200, Blair, NE 68009.

SHOPRULES

Is the future what it's cracked up to be?

If you've missed any LOOP titles, then here's your chance to order them!

#20201	GETTING IT TOGETHER: CJ by Wendy Corsi Staub	$3.50 U.S. ☐	$3.99 CAN. ☐
#20202	GETTING IT RIGHT: JESSICA by Carla Cassidy	$3.50 U.S. ☐	$3.99 CAN. ☐

(limited quantities available on certain titles)

TOTAL AMOUNT $ _____
POSTAGE & HANDLING $ _____
($1.00 for one book, 50¢ for each additional)
APPLICABLE TAXES* $ _____
TOTAL PAYABLE $ _____
(check or money order—please do not send cash)

To order, complete this form and send it, along with a check or money order for the total above, payable to Silhouette Books, to: **In the U.S.:** 3010 Walden Avenue, P.O. Box 9077, Buffalo, NY 14269-9077; **In Canada:** P.O. Box 636, Fort Erie, Ontario, L2A 5X3.

Name: _____
Address: _____ City: _____
State/Prov.: _____ Zip/Postal Code: _____

*New York residents remit applicable sales taxes.
Canadian residents remit applicable federal and provincial taxes.

Get smart. Get into "The Loop!"

Only from Silhouette®

where passion lives.

LOOPBL1